W9-AAA-882

the Tuckers

The Special Secret

By
Jo Mendel

Pictures by
Jackie Tomes

WHITMAN PUBLISHING COMPANY
RACINE, WISCONSIN

PRINTED IN U.S.A.

All names, characters, and events in this
story are entirely fictitious.

It's

Tucker

time!

The Wonderful House

The Tuckers find a real mystery when they move into the big old house on Valley View.

The Special Secret

Merry has a very special Fourth of July secret—and the Tuckers have a vacation they will never forget!

The Adventures of Plum Tucker

Uncle Roger plans exciting things to do every day while the Tuckers are in Oregon—but even Uncle Roger can't think of anything more exciting, more amazing, more just plain fun than—Plum Tucker.

Trouble on Valley View

No one knows where the trouble came from, but all the Tuckers know something has to be done about it. And each of them tries, in his own remarkable way!

CONTENTS

1	Fun for the Tuckers	11
2	The Milk-Carton Secret	21
3	Dive-Bombers!	38
4	Very Special Company!	56
5	Tent Town	73
6	Terry's Trick	92
7	Blondy and Muscle Man	105
8	A Trespasser	118
9	Thieves!	144
10	"Find My Feet!"	156
11	Mr. Wilson's Trouble	170
12	Playing Detective	186
13	Angry Tuckers	206
14	A Mystery-Puzzle	216
15	Fun—for Nobody!	234
16	The Smiths at Last	249
17	Floating Fire	267

1
Fun for the Tuckers

"Hey! There's a new boy on the beach!" Terry shouted as he loped past the open windows of Grandpa's summer cottage. The whole family was in the kitchen. That was the way nine-year-old Terry liked it. Tuckers all over the place!

Guiltily he saw that Merry, his twin, was practicing on her violin with her music propped against the sugar bowl. Merry's dark braids bounced every time she tapped her foot. Her nose wrinkled when a string squawked.

Father played solitaire on one corner of the long table. Grandpa mended fishing tackle. Between them Tom, the youngest Tucker, stood on his knees.

Terry could smell the vanilla in the cookies Mother, Grandma, and Tina were making. Grandma rolled and cut the dough. Tina placed the cookies on baking sheets. Mother Tucker guarded the oven.

Terry slammed the screen door. He skidded to a stop on Grandma's clean linoleum. He had not seen Penny playing paper dolls on the floor. In the confusion her dolls scattered.

"Sorry," he told Penny hastily. He dropped to his knees to help her pick up paper people and paper clothes.

Penny smiled. When Terry was around, if a thing was movable, it moved. "I'll just pretend a tornado," she told him.

"Swell!" Terry jumped to his feet. Rapidly he explained to anybody who would listen, "I've been swimming with a new kid. He's ten years old and his name is Butch, and—"

Merry whirled to face Terry. She punched the air with her violin bow and demanded, "Well, where does that leave *me*? Alone for the rest of vacation? When Grandpa invited us out here to Lake Annabelle, *you* said we would do everything together, remember? Everything!"

"But—" Terry sputtered. "But, but—"

"Oh, go oil your motor!" Merry retorted. "Has Butch a twin?"

"Sure," Father put in lazily. "He must have. And her name is Dutch."

Father winked at Grandpa, then showed Tom the card he turned. He grinned at Merry. "You know. Dutch and Butch, like Terry and Merry."

"Oh, Father!" Merry stamped a foot, but she giggled. "Imagine a twin named Dutch."

Terry was ready to grab any line that pulled him out of an argument with Merry. He whooped, "And Dutch's ears stick out, and she hasn't any eyebrows and—"

"None at all?" Penny asked anxiously.

"Butch's don't show," Terry said. He grinned at the picture he saw in his mind of a girl who looked as much like the new boy as he looked like Merry.

Merry must have read his mind. She said, "I'm glad your ears don't stick out, Terry Tucker."

Terry pushed his face close to hers. "And I'm

glad you don't have two big front teeth, Merry Tucker."

"Oh!" Penny cried with tenderhearted concern. "Does Butch even have big front teeth?"

"Two of 'em," Terry declared. He tapped his own solid teeth. "Right here. Looks like a bunny."

Tom shouted and drummed the table. "I like bunnies. I'll like Butch!"

Father put out a hand to guard his stack of cards. "Take it easy, Tom," he warned. "I might beat Old Solitaire this time."

Grandpa chuckled. "You're only beating because some cards moved out of place when Terry slammed the door and blew up that young typhoon."

Father shrugged good-naturedly.

Terry rescued Penny's favorite paper doll from Sugar, the cat. He hitched up a chair to watch Father's game. Sugar jumped into Terry's lap. He stroked the cat's black fur and smoothed his ragged ears.

Jealously Toby, the family's big dog, watched through the screen door. Toby thumped the porch with his tail. Then he stood on his hind legs and peered through the top half of the door.

Carrying Sugar, Terry let Toby in. Any pet belonging to a Tucker was a member of the family.

"Aw, why didn't you let yourself in?" Terry asked Toby. Toby just wiggled and dog-laughed.

"And don't you think Toby can't," Grandpa said. He rubbed the dog's shaggy head. Toby poked his nose against the edge of the table. "Toby's not so dumb. Has everybody waiting on him, hand and foot, when he can jolly well take care of himself."

"He's smart," Father said.

Toby knew he was being discussed. He left Grandpa and punched Father's elbow with his nose. A card dropped to the floor.

"See?" Father demanded. "I told you Toby's smart. See that card? He made me put it just where it belongs. I won!"

Everybody laughed.

Terry leaned back in his chair. He filled his lungs so full of air, he felt his ribs stretch. "Hey!" he burst out. "Why don't we vacation all the time? Right here in Grandpa's cottage on Lake Annabelle. This is—"

"—super," Tina said. Dreamily she patted her hand with the cooky spatula and walked to an open window overlooking the lake.

"Blow me down! Are you still on deck, matey?" Grandpa pretended to be surprised to find Tina in the room. She was eleven and eldest of the Tucker children. "I thought we had lost you overboard," he teased.

"Can't a fellow finish his own sentences around here?" Terry demanded.

"With five children in the family, you ask that?" Grandma twinkled at Terry. "Would you like a cooky?"

"I'll pass them," Tina offered quickly. She stacked a paper plate with warm cookies.

Merry reached for the first cooky. She took a big bite. Then she picked up her violin and began to tap one foot. Several times her bow scraped a string.

"I can't seem to get started on the right beat," she said. She wiggled her shoulders and arms in a way she called "putting her muscles in

place." She scowled at the music.

"Never mind, dear," Mother said soothingly. "Just keep trying."

"Well, O.K." Merry agreed. She brushed back a curl and put the violin under her chin. "If you can stand the noise, I can."

This time Merry started and kept going.

Penny nibbled the edge of her cooky. She fed the rest to Toby. Penny didn't have the appetite of the rest of the Tuckers. Busily she dressed her paper dolls. She bobbed her blond head and sang the Mexican song Merry played.

"La Cuca*ra*cha, la Cuca*ra*cha, *How* I ache in ev'ry *bone*. I'm tired of *walk*ing, I'm tired of *talk*-ing, *And* I wish to be a*lone*."

By the time Merry had played the song about the cockroach three times, all the Tuckers began to sing.

Toby stood on his hind feet and pranced. He tried to reach the cookies they waved to beat time.

Sugar liked quiet. He jumped off Terry's lap. He sat under Grandpa's chair to wash his ears and whiskers.

Suddenly Merry squeaked a string on a high note. "Mother, have we any empty paper milk cartons?" She grinned impishly at Mother's look of surprise. Mother was used to the clan's many projects and could be counted on to help. She was not often surprised.

"One or two," Mother answered. "Why?"

Merry's blue eyes sparkled. "Fourth of July is coming up," was the only reason she would give. "Just don't burn any cartons, please."

Terry was curious. He jerked his thumb toward the screen door to let Merry know he wanted to hear more about the milk cartons.

Merry wrinkled her nose and grinned. She turned her back and went on with her violin practice.

Terry knew Merry was getting even with him for swimming with the new boy while she practiced. Well, practicing was her own idea. She didn't have to do it during vacation. He tried to think up things she might do with milk cartons. None of his ideas seemed to have a thing to do with the Fourth of July. Milk cartons. Hmm.

Then Terry thought again about the new boy,

who seemed to have popped out of nowhere. Maybe Merry would like him when she got to know him. They could do things together. Tina and Merry were fun, of course, but Tom was not yet five. It would be good to have another boy around.

2
The Milk-Carton Secret

Terry squirmed with impatience while Merry and Tina put their heads together and whispered. "Merry, that's a super idea," Tina declared with a giggle. "But where will we get all those cartons?"

"We'll go around to all the cottages and gather them up," Merry planned. "Terry can help us carry them."

"Oh, I can, can I?" Terry burst out. "Not unless I know what they are for."

"Come on, Terry, be a good sport," Tina coaxed. "If everybody knows, the surprise will be spoiled."

"I'm not an everybody," Terry declared. He

folded his arms across his chest. "I'm Merry's twin. I can keep any secret Merry can think up."

"You won't tell that new boy?" Merry demanded.

"Cross my heart," Terry promised. He raised his right hand.

"I really didn't think it up, Terry," Merry confessed. "A girl I met on the beach told me about a Fourth of July without firecrackers at her camp. They saved all the waxed milk cartons from the camp kitchen. They waited till it was good and dark on the Fourth. Then they set the boxes afire and floated them down the middle of the lake. Everybody sang and watched the fires on the waves. Then they had a picnic."

"Will Mother think it's dangerous?" Terry asked doubtfully.

"Not if we go out in Grandpa's boat and light one carton at a time," Tina said. Generously she offered, "You can light the fires, Terry."

"Swell!" Terry said. "When do we start?"

"Right now!" Merry led the race down the shaded path and out of Grandpa's cottage yard.

Within a few minutes the Tuckers had tapped

on the back doors of all the neighbors' cottages. They returned to Grandpa's porch with only nine waxed paper cartons.

Merry's forehead puckered. "That's not enough."

"But everybody promised to save cartons for us," Tina reminded.

"We'll need at least a hundred cartons for a good show," Merry insisted. "Who drinks that much milk?"

They sat in a row on the porch steps and stared at the nine cartons.

"It would have been fun," Merry mourned. "I wanted to invite all the neighbors and have a great big wiener roast, just like they did at that camp."

"Yes," Tina said, sighing.

Glumly Terry studied his sisters' faces. Tina was tall, slim, and blond, with a face so sensitive every thought showed. Usually she helped the younger Tuckers out of their problems. Terry saw that Tina was trying hard to think up some way to make Merry's plan work.

Penny was like Tina, Terry thought, as he

turned his attention to his youngest sister. She worked on a dandelion chain near the porch. When her chain needed extra length, Penny climbed over the fence and picked some yellow dandelions from a neighbor's grass.

Suddenly Terry snapped his fingers. "I have it! We'll do what Penny is doing."

"Pick dandelions?" Merry asked disgustedly. "Fine thing."

"Of course not." Terry was too much interested in his own plan to argue with Merry. "I mean, let's not be stopped because the cartons aren't right here. Let's borrow Grandpa's boat and go around the bay. I'll bet we'll collect a lot of cartons."

"Let's!" Tina and Merry agreed instantly.

Merry ran to the picnic table under the cottonwoods. There the grown-up Tuckers talked with neighbors and watched Tom on the beach. "Remember your life jackets," Dad reminded.

Tina helped Terry attach a small motor to the Tub, the sailboat which Grandpa had built himself.

The Tub was a banana-shaped boat with

removable rigging. It was built for safety, not speed. It moved as slowly as a log in the waves when oars or motor were used. But when rigged for sailing, it scudded at a fast clip over the roughest water on Lake Annabelle. Once Grandpa weathered a wind so severe the rigging came down in a tangle of sails and rope, mast and boom. The float tanks under the bow and stern seats allowed the sturdy Tub to ride out the storm.

The Tuckers trusted Grandpa's boat. Grandpa trusted in their sense of responsibility.

Grandpa had been in the Navy long ago. From

Tina to Tom he was training the Tuckers to take care of themselves in water. For two years Tina, Merry, and Terry had been permitted to row near shore while an adult watched. Each could now swim forty yards without resting. Each knew a small piece of wood held up a person in water. They could float with or without their life preservers. Finally this summer had come when Grandpa allowed them to use the motor out of sight of the cottage.

"*Bon voyage!*" Mother called.

Tina, Merry, and Terry waved. They shouted across the water at Tom until he was doll-size in the distance.

Terry sat in the stern to steer. Merry and Tina dangled their hands overboard. They pushed through the waves not much faster than a man can walk—fast enough to feel wind in their faces, but slow enough to watch the shore.

"Don't go out too far," Tina reminded. "We would waste time going back when we find a house."

When they reached a dock in front of a group of cottages, Terry waited in the boat. Tina and

Merry ran along paths and knocked on doors. They returned with five cartons.

"Nine and five," Merry counted. "Fourteen!"

Within an hour they had collected a stack of cartons in the bow of the Tub.

"I think we've been gone long enough," Tina decided. "Mother might worry."

"But we don't have a hundred boxes," Merry objected.

"Everybody promised to save more for us," Tina reminded.

Terry turned in a wide circle and headed back home.

"Somebody is waving," Merry said. "See? Over by that bathhouse."

"That's Butch!" Terry declared. "Let's pick him up."

"Should we?" Tina worried. "Grandpa hasn't said anything about picking up people."

"He didn't say we couldn't, did he?" Terry argued.

"No," Tina agreed doubtfully.

"Well, O.K.," Terry said in a tone that put an end to the matter. "I'm going to pick him up."

"If Butch asks questions, don't explain about our cartons," Merry warned. "You promised."

When Terry beached the boat, Butch climbed into the Tub. Tina and Merry grinned at each other. Butch was just as colorless as Terry had described him. White crew cut, pale eyebrows, gray eyes, untanned skin, and big ears were not a pretty combination.

"That's Tina," Terry told Butch. "She's eleven. And that's Merry. She's nine, same as I am."

Butch looked from Terry to Merry and back again. "You're twins," he said.

Merry giggled at his solemn surprise.

"Where shall I drop you off?" Terry tried to sound like Father.

Butch waved his hands. "Uh, anywhere."

"Well, where do you live?" Merry asked.

"Uh," was all Butch said. He stared over the top of a row of young birches.

Terry carefully pushed off and pulled the cord of the motor. After three tugs, the motor started and he headed into the bay.

"We know most of the people at this end of

the lake," Merry said, trying to be helpful. "What's your last name?"

"Smith," Butch said.

None of the three Tuckers knew any Smiths on Lake Annabelle.

"What does your house look like?" Tina asked.

"Uh," Butch said, "it's square and has a porch."

"And windows and doors!" Merry added with a giggle.

"Merry, don't tease," Tina cautioned, but she grinned. "We're not being nosy, Butch," she explained. "Terry won't know where to take you unless you tell us where you live."

"Oh-oh." The motor *sput-sputted*, and Terry pushed the lever to shut off the motor. "Now it doesn't matter where Butch lives. I can't take him home."

"What's wrong, Terry?" Merry asked anxiously.

"Out of gas."

"Oh!" Tina gasped. With her eyes she measured their distance from shore and the depth of the water. "We're a long way out."

"We can row," Terry said. Carefully he stood up and moved to the seat beside Butch. "Move over," he told the new boy. "We came out by horsepower, but we have to go home by boy power!"

It was soon obvious to the Tuckers that Butch had never used oars. He was so slow about setting his oar in its lock, Tina said, "You'd better put it in, Terry."

"Uh, I can do it," Butch insisted, but Terry reached to help him. With four hands on the same oar, it fell overboard.

Tina tried to save the oar. The rocking of the boat pushed it beyond her fingers.

Clumsily Terry turned the boat with one oar. But each time Tina reached, the oar slid over the top of the next lazy wave.

"What are we going to do?" Merry asked excitedly.

"I'm going to swim for the oar," Tina said. She stood up and tugged at her padded life jacket.

"You know you're not allowed to take off that

life jacket!" Merry reminded.

"Well, she can't dive with it on," Terry said.

"I won't take off my jacket. I'll just tumble in," Tina said practically.

Terry helped Tina to balance on the rim of the rocking boat. Overboard she splashed. When she shook the water out of her eyes, Tina could not see the oar. "Where is it?" she shouted.

Merry pointed toward the north shore. "It's going that-away!" she shouted back.

Yelling and pointing, Merry and Terry kept Tina on course. But the oar was always just ahead. With the padded jacket on, Tina could not flatten out into a fast crawl. And she did not dare take it off. It was up to her to return to the boat. The Tub could not come for her.

Reluctantly she turned.

Terry and Merry stood on their knees to help Tina bounce on the water. When she rolled into the boat, Tina was near tears. "I just couldn't catch up," she said. She put her head down on her folded arms to rest.

After Tina had rested, Terry said, "We can't sit here all day."

"Well, do you have any bright ideas?" Merry asked pertly.

Terry snapped his fingers. "We'll push the boat to shore."

"Oh, sure!" Merry bobbed her head. "We'll just get out and wade!"

"Don't be silly. You know I mean swim-push." Terry stood up, prepared to go overboard. "Tina can steer. Butch and I will push."

"Uh," Butch said, turning red. He looked at the water. He did not move.

"Butch doesn't have a life jacket," Tina reminded Terry, to help the new boy out of an embarrassing spot. She knew he was afraid.

"Then that leaves me," Merry said briskly.

The twins splashed into position on either side of the Tub, just back of the rowing seat. Tina climbed onto the bow. There she sat cross-legged. It was not easy to handle the oar like a canoe paddle, but Tina refused to leave all the work to Merry and Terry. Slowly, slowly the boat edged toward shore.

Tina's arms were so tired she was afraid she would drop the oar, but it was useless to expect help from Butch. He sat in the very middle of the boat and stared at sky and water.

They came to shore in a place where wild rice grew. Red-winged blackbirds flew away. An old turtle dived and left bubbles on the surface of the water.

"Ugh," Merry gritted her teeth when her feet tangled in weeds. "Maybe there are water snakes."

"Maybe there are," Terry teased.

"I'll scream!" Merry warned.

"If there are snakes I'll biff them over the head with the oar," Tina promised.

"And lose our only oar?" Merry shrieked. "Don't you dare!"

The twins waded and pulled the boat up on a pebbly beach. Quickly, Tina jumped ashore. "Coming, Butch?" she asked.

"Uh, what are we going to do?" Butch wanted to know.

"Find something to row with, of course," Terry said. "Let's scatter and search."

Not so much as a scrap of board had been found when the group met again at the boat.

"But I saw a path!" Merry exclaimed.

"Well, a path goes someplace. What are we waiting for?" Terry demanded. "If there's a house at the end of this path, its owners must be midgets," he declared as they pushed through overhanging boughs and cobwebs.

"Or just a cottage owner who hasn't had his vacation yet," Tina corrected sensibly.

Within a few minutes they discovered a fishing shack. They went completely around the building. An ax had rusted all winter in a chopping block. Ruefully Terry said, "It's a sure thing we can't row with an ax."

"But we might use a broom," Tina suggested. She picked up an old broom which had lost half its straws.

"Yeah," Terry said. He grinned broadly. "Let's go test it."

Rowing with a broom was awkward, but possible. The Tuckers took turn-about since the straws became so heavy with water the rower soon tired. They sang Grandpa's navy songs and Mitchell Grade School's pep yells.

"Land, ho!" Merry shrieked when they came in sight of their own beach.

Soon a motorboat put out from the boat dock. As it came near, they saw that Grandpa and Father were in their neighbor Mr. Pitcher's boat.

"Aren't they beautiful?" Merry sighed blissfully. Butch looked surprised that she considered the men in her family beautiful. She giggled and teased, "I look just like them. Of course, they are pretty!"

"Conceited goon," Terry muttered, but he grinned. Father and Grandpa looked pretty good to him, too, after the struggle to get home. "We'll hunt for the oar tomorrow, Grandpa," Terry promised, worried because he had lost borrowed property.

"There are extra oars in the shed," Grandpa assured them.

But they looked at each other, making a silent promise to find the oar they had borrowed and lost.

"And we didn't lose one milk carton!" Merry said triumphantly.

On shore they had a story to tell, and some questions to answer about how they had handled the emergency.

Tina was the only one to see Butch slide away from the group. With a puzzled frown she watched him run down the beach. He seemed headed for the spot where they had first picked him up. "He's a funny boy," she muttered.

3

Dive-Bombers!

Loaded with waxed milk cartons, the five Tuckers dumped their boxes in Grandpa's back yard.

"Where are you going to keep them?" Terry asked Merry. "Above your bunk?"

Merry, Mother, Tina, and Penny slept in their old vacation trailer parked near Grandpa's back door. Dad and the boys shared a sleeping porch over the kitchen. In crowded quarters there was certainly no room for a stack of milk cartons.

Merry covered her mouth with one hand and widened her eyes. "I didn't think of that," she admitted. "They certainly take up a lot of room, don't they?"

"You can put some in the shelf over my bed," Penny offered generously.

Tina hugged Penny's shoulders. "Thanks, honey," she said. "Terry was teasing." Penny, who was seven, was the only frail member of the Tucker family. Since she was often sick, the rest of the children petted her more than they did each other.

Tom had been walking around the boxes. Now he examined them from all sides. "These are good stackin' stuff," he said. "I can make a swell wall." He set to work lining up boxes along the back porch wall.

Merry gave Tom an affectionate swat on his seat. "You just build a wall," she said. "A nice neat one that Grandma won't ask us to tear down." Free of her problem, Merry whirled with a gypsy-swish of her dark braids. "Who's for a swim? I've had so much milk dripped on me, my clothes smell like a cheese factory!"

"Last one in is a Swiss cheese!" Terry yelled. He led the race for bathing suits.

When Merry awoke early the next morning, she heard a smack! smack! smack! Quickly she hobbled barefoot across the yard. At the kitchen door she found Grandma waving her apron and saying, "Shoo! Shoo!" while Mother waved a fly swatter. At least a hundred yellow jackets buzzed around the kitchen door.

Merry dodged one of the insects. "Did Toby drag a dead fish up from the beach?" she squealed.

"Not dead fish," Mother answered crisply. "Sour milk!" Mother crept up on a yellow jacket that had found its way through a loose screen. "Merry, I don't know what you are planning, and whatever it is, you know I'll help if I can—but! We must be able to open the kitchen door without being dive-bombed!"

Merry gulped, "Yes, ma'am." Hurriedly she told Mother, "I'll go wake Terry to help me move those boxes."

In a few minutes Terry and Tom let themselves out through the front door and circled the house. There they stood in a row with Tina, Merry, and Penny and considered their problem.

"We'll get stung if we try to carry those

boxes anywhere," Tina worried.

"I could make a cone trap," Terry suggested.

"Before breakfast?" Merry asked. "I'm hungry."

"W-Well, no," Terry admitted.

"I can move those boxes," Tom said sturdily. "I'll do it." He disappeared to return with Grandpa's big spray gun. Tom pumped clouds of insect-killer into the air and walked bravely into the swirl of yellow jackets. The spray did not kill the wasps, but it did slow them.

Terry recognized Tom's plan. "Cover me, Tom!" he ordered, talking out of the side of his mouth like a television gangster. "I'll grab those boxes."

"Me, too!" Merry volunteered.

While Tom pumped spray, Terry, Merry, and Tina ran back and forth from the porch to the lean-to shed hooked onto the garage. Behind the shed, the boxes would be out of sight. A few hungry insects followed to make dive-bomb raids on the new food supply they had found.

When the last box was removed from the porch, Grandma came through the door with a pail of hot soapy water and a mop.

Merry ran across the yard. "I'll clean the porch, Grandma!" she called.

At that moment Grandpa crossed the yard with a string of bass. "This beats all! I must be getting deaf. Merry, I thought I heard you offer to mop."

Merry flipped her fingers when she waved. "This mess was my fault," she confessed.

"Now about those cartons—" Grandpa raised a questioning eyebrow. He jerked his thumb toward the pile where Terry and Tom had made another wall.

Merry grinned. "I'm not talking, Grandpa. It's a secret."

After breakfast Terry and Tom worked busily with scrap screen-wire and string. While Tina and Merry washed dishes, they installed a cone of wire on a stump in the back yard.

Tom bustled in and rummaged a cupboard while Tina folded towels.

"We need some jam," Tom said. His cheeks and ears were pink with his sense of importance.

"Bread, too?" Tina asked, puzzled.

"Just jam," Tom told her and hurried out of the kitchen.

By the middle of the morning the boys' trap, baited with jam, was filled with angry yellow jackets. Now it was safe to use the kitchen door. Tom was so interested in the wasps that he patrolled the yard with the big spray gun. He even refused to go swimming.

As they ran down the path, pulling on bathing caps, Tina told Merry, "The waves look like pleats in the water today."

Sun-sparkles on the edges of the waves moved so fast they looked like tiny raindrops of light.

Butterflies fanned wings while they rested on damp sand. A bass slapped shallow water near a sun-bleached log. Motors of boats droned. Several boats were pulled up on shore. Once in a while heat expansion of a gas tank made the cracking sound of gunshot. In the distance a dog barked.

Penny dog-paddled for a few minutes, then worked on a sand castle. Merry and Tina floated on big black inner tubes.

"Isn't this fun?" Merry asked blissfully. She turned her face to the sky and felt the sun warm even her eyelashes.

"Yes," Tina agreed. "But what's the matter with Grandma?"

"Grandma?" Merry sputtered. She sat up so suddenly she almost sat through her inner tube. "Did she fall in the lake?"

"No, silly. She's sitting on that log under the cottonwoods on the beach. See?" Tina pointed. "See how funny she's acting? Jerking and moving back and forth on the log?"

Merry pushed heavy, wet hair out of her eyes. She had been too impatient to swim to tuck her

hair under her bathing cap.

Anxiously, both girls watched Grandma. She wore a huge beach hat of woven palm fronds. It was trimmed with bright fruit and flowers. Every few seconds she took off the hat and put it on again. Each time Grandma examined her hat, she moved to another section of the log.

"Maybe the yellow jackets are after those big red whatchamacallit flowers," Merry suggested with a giggle.

"Merry, how can you laugh about that?" Tina asked seriously. "Let's go see what's wrong."

"You go," Merry retorted lazily. "If you get

stung, I'll know it was yellow jackets." She lay back on her inner tube. She reached out both arms to paddle with her hands.

Tina rolled off her tube and started swimming for shore.

"Brr!" Merry shouted. "You kicked water on me!"

"That's to punish you for being so hard-hearted!" Tina retorted.

"I'm not hardhearted. I'm just sensible. I know Grandma wouldn't sit there and let herself be stung."

Tina was used to taking care of the rest of the family. She could not enjoy the cool water of Lake Annabelle when Grandma was uncomfortable.

When she reached the shore-end of the boat-dock, Tina dropped her feet to the bottom and waded. Her slim, tall body cast a thin shadow on the sand.

"Are you all right, Grandma?" she called.

"Don't try to run, child," Grandma answered. "Your feet are still tender from wearing shoes all winter. Sit down." She patted the log.

Tina felt a bit silly, now that she sat beside Grandma. No yellow jackets flew around Grandma's big hat. No red ants crawled in the bark of the log. A bumblebee droned, but it sounded happy and busy. Tina laughed with embarrassment. "I guess I'm just a worrywart. I thought something was wrong."

The fine wrinkles deepened around Grandma's young-looking blue eyes. She faced Tina in order to look out from under her huge hat.

"Now that you mention it, child," Grandma said, "there *is* something odd going on. My hat has been hit several times. I can't discover who is doing it. Penny is building a sand castle. Your grandfather and Terry are out there at the end of the dock putting up the sails on the Tub. Your parents are sun-bathing on the dock. And you and Merry were floating."

Grandma shook her head till the palm fronds rattled. "Tom is herding wasps in the yard. There's nobody else. It must have been my imagination."

Something stung Tina's back. "Oh, no, it wasn't your imagination!" She jumped up and turned her back to Grandma. "Is there a bug on my back?"

"Just a tiny red spot."

"I wasn't stung. I was *hit!*" Tina declared. Slowly she turned. She stared at clumps of tall green grass and blooming forget-me-nots which pushed up through the sand. Then she looked at the birches and cottonwoods. Nobody was in sight. "Well, that beats all," she said, using one of Grandpa's pet phrases.

"Hey, Butch!" Terry called from the boat-dock. His voice sounded thin and far away, even when he was close enough for Tina to see his hands cupped like a megaphone.

There was no answer.

"I think I've had enough sun," Grandma announced. "I'll go up to the cottage and make a pitcher of lemonade."

"I'll help," Tina offered, glad for the chance to work in the kitchen with Grandma. Grandma Tucker was one of the best cooks in Yorkville where they lived on the opposite shore of Lake Annabelle. It was Tina's ambition to learn Grandma's secrets.

Tina opened the kitchen door for Grandma. She stood aside for her to enter. Just as she turned, Tina saw a jiggle of boughs in one of the tall cottonwoods. A boy slid to the ground. Almost at once she saw Terry run down the dock to meet Butch. Together they hurried back to the sailboat where Grandpa waited. Puzzled, Tina glanced from the tree to the dock. How had Butch crossed that sand without her seeing him? Up in the tree one minute, on the dock the next. It didn't make sense. Tina's lips folded. No matter how he made himself invisible, Butch should not flip pebbles at old ladies.

Tina was not a person to put things off. She had something to say to this new boy, and right now! "Excuse me, Grandma," she called.

Down the shady path she ran, across the pebbles and over the sand. Over the catwalk and down the length of the boat-dock her long legs sped. She narrowly missed stepping on Father's foot when she passed her sun-bathing parents. "Oops," she said. "Excuse me." She came to an abrupt halt in front of Terry, the new boy, and Grandpa Tucker.

"What are you doing here, Butch?" Tina snapped.

"Blow me down, matey!" Grandpa said with surprise. "Is Butch a barnacle to be scraped off the dock?"

Tina's chin lifted. Her smooth blond hair swung against the points of her sunburned shoulders. "Why should I be polite to Butch? He threw rocks at Grandma!"

"I did not!" Butch denied hotly. "I've never thrown a rock at an old lady in my life."

"You did!" Tina insisted. "Just now, under the cottonwood."

Terry squared off in front of Butch. "So you did throw rocks, huh?"

"No!" Butch declared.

"Now, now, mateys," Grandpa cautioned. "Butch says he didn't throw rocks, so there must be some mistake."

Tina could still feel the stinging place on her back. Somebody had flipped pebbles. And if that somebody was not Butch, who was it? There was nobody else on the beach.

"You just leave Grandma alone if you want

to be friends with us Tuckers," Tina warned Butch.

"Yeah," Terry agreed.

Butch just muttered, "Uh, sure," and looked into space. He looked so miserable, Tina was almost sorry she had spoken.

"Step lively, mateys. Put on your life jackets and come aboard the Tub," Grandpa invited. "There's a good breeze going to waste." Love of wind and water was in Grandpa's bones.

Soon the Tub began to ride the waves, pushed by wind.

"Nothing like a spanking breeze to float away what frets you," Grandpa said contentedly.

Tina agreed with him. When the canvas filled and the boat gained speed, she turned her face into the spray. Faster and faster they sped, with no *put-put* of motor or splash of oars to break the magic. An occasional creak and squeak of mast, spars and boom, gurgle of water in the well, and sigh and snap of sail made music a Tucker could understand.

Tina leaned toward Terry and pointed at a duck which flew overhead. The bird's pale feet were tucked back close to its body.

Terry tipped his head and shaded his eyes. "Good design for a landing gear," he said.

A fish flipped up to snatch an insect from the air. Spreading rings of water showed the place it had been. Then the boat broke the rings. A long V of wake-water stretched toward shore. Dreamily Tina told Terry, "The water looks like lime gelatin that hasn't quite set."

"While you're looking at the gelatin, remember to watch for the oar we lost," Terry reminded.

Happily Grandpa began to rumble in his throat. Tina and Terry knew just when to shout, "Yo, heave ho!" in Grandpa's song.

But Tina became aware that Butch had slid to the floorboards and was huddled in a tight ball. He watched every movement of Grandpa's wrinkled hands. Plainly Butch was not having fun.

Tina dodged the boom as they came about. She asked Butch, "What's the matter? Do you get seasick?"

Butch shook his head. He clawed at the cracks

between the floorboards. "Wh-what if we turn over?" he asked fearfully.

"We'd swim, of course!" Terry hooted.

Tina forgot that Butch was almost as old as she and must have flipped pebbles at Grandma, even though he denied it. He was somebody who needed help.

"That's what our life jackets are for," she told Butch.

Terry looked a little scornful. "The Tub won't roll," he said.

Grandpa ran parallel with the long north shore of Lake Annabelle. Cottages sat on slopes, each with its boat-dock poking out from the beach. Fishermen, in anchored boats, rocked on the waves. Water skiers skimmed behind speedboats down the middle of the lake. A few sails were white patches against the blue sky. Even before they had moved to Yorkville, from Castleton, the Tuckers had spent week ends and vacations on Lake Annabelle with Grandma and Grandpa. Tina knew every twist and turn of the shoreline.

Suddenly she sat up straight. "What was that?" she asked.

"Did you see the oar we lost?" Terry asked at once.

Tina pointed at a boxlike white house with many windows and much latticework painted red. "No, I thought I saw somebody at the Arney house."

"Pooh," Terry scoffed. "You're seeing things. Arneys always come to the lake in August."

"But I did see something," Tina insisted. She happened to be facing Butch at that moment. He, too, was looking at the red and white house. There was a tight line around his mouth.

4
Very Special Company!

When she poured the breakfast coffee the next morning, Grandma beamed at Father and Grandpa. "My!" she sighed happily. "I feel lucky to have both of you on vacation at the same time."

"It isn't a matter of luck," Grandpa declared with a wink at Father. "We're smart. We hire good help at the store." He pushed back his chair. "Looks like a fine day to paint the window trim."

"O.K. with me," Father said good-naturedly. "We have to do some work to appreciate playtime. We'll be spruced up for the Fourth." He grinned at Tom, who sat beside him. "Isn't that right, son?" he asked.

"I'll stir the paint," Tom offered so quickly he choked on a bite of toast.

Father slapped Tom's back. "Think you'll live, Tom?" he asked when Tom recovered.

Tom nodded. Hastily he reached for his milk.

Gravely Father told Tom, "Thanks for the offer, old man. But I was just about to suggest a boat ride."

Tom was no pouter. For a minute he looked disappointed. Then he stood up and told the rest of the Tuckers, "Meet you on the dock."

Tina and Merry helped Grandpa furl the sails. Terry snapped the lock of the guard chain when Grandpa put the motor on the Tub. Terry stepped from the dock to the stern of the boat. He wound the starting cord on the outboard motor.

"My turn to steer," Tina reminded Terry. "And it's Penny's turn to choose where we go."

In her padded life jacket Penny looked like a pixie. She flushed with pleasure and pointed at the deep woods. They stretched south of Grandpa's cottage to meet the blue sky in the distance.

"South it is," Tina agreed. "Shove off, Terry."

"Aye, aye!" Terry saluted. He used an oar to

push the boat free of the dock. He plopped onto the center seat by an oarlock. Accusingly he told Tina, "We're wasting time. We won't find milk cartons in the woods."

"We'll hunt for cartons later," Tina said calmly. She smiled at Penny to let her know they would motor past the woods.

"Next time I'll wash the cartons and spray 'em *before* I stack 'em," Tom said wisely.

On this side of the lake the shore was ragged. Tina steered carefully to miss sunken logs and hidden rocks.

Once a kingfisher gave his rattling cry and dived for a fish. Shore birds teetered along the sand.

"Oh-oh," Penny gasped and pointed.

In a tiny cove Tina saw two baby skunks. They walked shoulder to shoulder like school children marching to class. Tina stopped the boat to let Tom and Penny watch them. The skunks lapped water like kittens. Then they marched away. They held their striped tails as stiff as flags.

Merry pointed at a wisp of smoke which rose

behind some young willows. "Somebody must be building a new cottage."

Terry squinted and frowned. "No. Grandpa and I went around the whole lake a couple of days ago. There is nothing new."

A little anxiously the Tuckers watched the smoke. Fire and water were both friends and enemies of cottage owners. Tina circled the willows and headed for shore. While she beached the Tub, she saw a white-haired boy run into some bushes. A small fire burned near a stone.

"Wasn't that Butch?" Tina asked Terry.

"I don't think so," Terry said. "Butch would have waved."

"I don't care who it was," Merry said indignantly. "I'm going to count my milk cartons when I get home. See what he's burning!"

Merry pointed. Cartons were stacked against the rock. Several boxes burned under a fish on a stick.

Terry sniffed the air. "Smells good. Let's catch some perch and have a cook-out."

"Not now. I want to go home."

Merry sounded so determined, Tina swung

the Tub in a wide curve. She headed north again. With her last glimpse of the little cove, Tina was sure she saw the boy return to the fire. If that boy was Butch, he had lost weight overnight!

At Grandpa's dock, Merry was first out of the Tub. She ran up the path while Terry snapped the mooring chain. Tina helped Penny take off her life jacket and turned to help Tom.

"I can do it!" he insisted.

Tina followed Merry to the carton stack behind the shed.

"This beats all!" Merry declared. "I counted and they are all here. I don't understand it. Why did that boy stack those cartons? Floating fire was *my* idea!" When Tina could not explain, Merry demanded, "Do you know anybody else who saves cartons?"

Tina had to admit that a wall of cartons was unusual. It was doubly unusual to find two walls on the same lake on the same day.

Merry stuck out her lower lip and bobbed her head solemnly. "I think we have a mystery on our hands."

"The Mystery of the Missing Cartons," Tina

MILK
MILK
MILK
MILK
MILK
MILK

said, letting her imagination play with the title. "Who dun-it?"

"Butch!" Merry insisted.

"There isn't any mystery if you already know the answer!" Tina objected.

A horn honked. Both girls turned to watch the milk truck drive into the parking lot. Tom came from the dock just in time to meet the milkman. "More milk cartons, Merry!" Tom yelled.

Terry was right behind Tom. "Hi, Mr. Wilson!" Terry shouted. "Are you alone today?"

"Sure am, Terry. Would you like a delivery job? I pay off in ice-cream bars." Mr. Wilson took off his striped cap. He pushed back his hair. His forehead was white, while the rest of his face was weathered brown. The milkman sounded businesslike, but smile lines crinkled the corners of his eyes.

"You've hired yourself a man," Terry agreed at once. "Give me a minute to ask Father."

"I want to go, too!" Merry insisted.

"Me, too," Tina called.

Riding with the milkman was one of the adventures the Tuckers enjoyed each summer on Lake Annabelle. It gave them a chance to greet old friends and meet new ones. Not many people moved into their summer homes before the Fourth of July. But today there were enough milk deliveries to keep them busy.

One customer waited with a fat baby in a stroller. A sign above the gate read GREEN FIELDS.

"Hello, Mrs. Fields," Mr. Wilson called. "How is my youngest customer?"

Proudly Mrs. Fields lifted the baby. "Wilson Dairy products agree with him, don't you think, Mr. Wilson?"

When they left Mrs. Fields, Mr. Wilson was humming under his breath. "Nothing like a satisfied customer to make a man feel good," he told the Tuckers.

"That's what Father and Grandpa say when they have a good day at Tuckers' Town Talk," Terry said. He leaned far out of the truck to stare at some mailboxes by the side of the road. "Got many customers?"

"A pretty good route," Mr. Wilson answered.

"Anybody named Smith?"

Mr. Wilson thought for a minute. "Nobody named Smith," he declared.

Terry, Merry, and Tina exchanged puzzled glances.

"Maybe Butch doesn't like milk," Merry said, shrugging.

"You lost me," Mr. Wilson told Merry with a grin. "Who's Butch?"

"That's what we'd like to know," Merry retorted.

Terry told about meeting the new boy who said his name was Smith.

"He must know his own name," Mr. Wilson said drily. He jerked his thumb at a mailbox. "How about checking the boxes?"

"That's what I've been doing," Terry said. "There is no new box and nobody named Smith."

"I give up," Mr. Wilson said.

But the tilt of Terry's chin let Tina and Merry know Terry was not going to give up until he found out where Butch Smith lived and why he didn't tell.

After the milk was delivered, the return trip through the summer colony was a fast one. Mr.

Wilson stopped the truck where a short-cut path connected the road with Grandpa's parking lot. The milkman gave them chocolate-coated ice-cream bars. He handed a bag to Tina. "A treat for Tom and Penny," he said. "And a quart of vanilla for your folks."

They hurried through the woods to share the ice cream before it melted. Merry said, "I hear voices in the parking lot."

A big laugh rang out.

"Uncle Fred!" Tina shouted. She raced around the corner of the shed. "Uncle Fred, when did you come?"

"Just got here." Uncle Fred nodded at his car parked beside Father's blue station wagon. He mopped his face with a bandana. "Ninety-five in the shade at the farm," he declared. "Hot enough to send anybody to water."

"We have some ice cream to cool you off," Tom said.

"Where's Aunt Anne?" Tina and Merry demanded.

"Went in the house with her basket." Uncle Fred's voice let them know there was something special in that basket. There always was! Uncle Fred and Aunt Anne lived on a dairy farm in the northern part of the state.

"What did she bring to eat?" Merry asked.

"Wait and see," Uncle Fred teased.

Tom hurried from the parking lot. He carried two overnight bags when one would have been a big load.

"Let me give you a hand, young man," Uncle Fred said.

Tom said importantly, "Father is putting away the paint cans. He says 'hurry it up.' We're going swimming."

"You tell him that's what I came for," Uncle Fred declared.

In a very few minutes the whole family gathered at the beach.

White sand made a clean carpet under water just the right depth for safety. Although Aunt Anne was roly-poly from eating her own good cooking, she joined a game of water ball. She swam as well as Father, who was her brother.

Father and Uncle Fred raced to the line of logs which formed a boom to protect the swimming area. Then Uncle Fred challenged Father to a tug of war.

"Been saving up my strength, Bill Tucker," Uncle Fred crowed. He made such big muscles in his arms, Tom had to touch them.

"You'd better watch it, Father," Tom warned. "Uncle Fred is strong!"

"So you think I'm a sissy!" Father scoffed.

As a dairy farmer, Uncle Fred was used to hard work. But so was Father. He and Grandpa owned a small variety store in Yorkville, and Father handled big boxes of stock. Father also exercised during week ends at the cottage.

Both men scooped small trenches in the sand for their feet. Terry brought a rope from the Tub. Grandpa tied knots in the ends of the rope. Each man held a knot. They faced each other, alert and ready to take the dare.

Grandpa marked a center line. He took his handkerchief from his hip pocket.

All the Tuckers lined up on the sand in cheering sections. When Grandpa's handkerchief hit the ground, Father and Uncle Fred began to pull. They doubled up. They leaned back till their bodies slanted. They worked! Uncle Fred's face got redder and redder. His gray hair looked like a wig set on a young head.

Father grunted. Muscles made knots in his arms.

The rope was a tight line between the two men. Once Uncle Fred pulled Father till his feet slid.

"Work, Father!" Tina shrieked. "You almost touched the center line!"

"Hooray, Uncle Fred!" Terry yelled.

Merry bounced back and forth, not sure which man she wanted to win.

Backward and forward, the men skidded.

Finally Uncle Fred caught Father off balance. He began a steady pull.

Seeing that Father was losing, Tina darted behind him. She grabbed him around the waist. "Help me, Merry!" she shouted.

Instantly the family divided into two laughing, pulling lines. When Uncle Fred's team won, everybody fell in the sand.

Tom jumped up and brushed sand from his red bathing trunks. "Let's do it again. That was fun!"

"I'm winded," Father declared. "Pull with Penny, Tom."

Tom's eyes swept across Penny's small shoulders. "I'd hurt her," he said. Penny was two years older than Tom. She was taller, but he weighed more.

"Let's choose sides," Merry said. "Captain!"

"Captain!" Tom shouted.

Butch showed up just in time to even up the sides. Tom chose Tina and Butch.

"That won't make it even," Merry said, weighing teams with her eyes. "Tina, you take my place as captain. I'll be on Tom's team."

"Yay, team!" Terry chanted. "Let's go!"

They pulled so hard they almost sat in the sand. But neither side could win.

"It's a draw," Terry declared. "Let's eat."

"Mother," Aunt Anne told Grandma, "don't go near the kitchen. I brought a picnic."

Tom ran up the path for Grandma's plastic tablecloth. Mother spread it on the large beach table.

Tom sat closest to the lunch basket. He watched Aunt Anne unpack a juicy pink ham, crusty loaves of new bread, creamy cottage cheese, fried chicken, and a red cherry cobbler. Uncle Fred carried a tall can of ice-cold buttermilk from his car.

Merry and Tina placed the plates and silver. Terry held a tray of glasses for Uncle Fred to fill.

"Come, look!" Terry shouted.

Penny, Tom, Merry, and Tina peered into the big can. A lump of country butter floated on the cold milk.

"There's maple syrup to go with that butter for breakfast," Aunt Anne told them. She glowed with cheerful pride in the food she had provided.

"I thought Grandma was the world's best cook," Terry said, sniffing hungrily. "Now I don't know."

Grandpa laid an arm across Aunt Anne's plump shoulders. "My Annie learned her mother's cooking secrets," he said proudly.

"Mother knows them, too," Penny said loyally. "And Tina is learning."

After lunch the family lounged in the cottage yard. The grownups used the comfortable lawn furniture. The children spread their beach towels in the shade.

Butch had no towel. He sat a little apart. His white skin was splotched with sunburn almost as red as his striped trunks. His pale hair stuck up in wisps.

"Come share my towel," Terry invited.

Butch stretched out beside Terry, but he was obviously listening to every word Uncle Fred said. Terry listened idly. He wondered why Butch was so interested. Uncle Fred was just talking about grubbing out roots for a new pasture for his dairy cattle.

5
Tent Town

In a little silence Grandma said, "We'll have to plan for bed space tonight."

"Now, Mother, don't you worry," Aunt Anne said quietly. "Fred and I brought folding cots and sleeping bags. We'll just sleep out here in the yard and love it."

Father raised himself on one elbow. "Are you trying to make me feel selfish, sis? I'll give you my bed on the porch."

Penny had been half asleep. Now she asked, "But where will you sleep, Father?"

"In the trailer. I'll just move you out in the yard, Penny," Father teased.

Terry jumped up. He yelled, "Hey, could we?"

Father looked at him, puzzled.

"Could you what?"

"Could we sleep out in the yard?"

Father stretched and yawned. "I don't know why not," he said.

Terry punched Butch in the ribs. "Want to sleep with me, Butch? We'll go ask your mother."

"Uh, sure," Butch agreed. Then hastily he added, "But I'll go ask her. You don't have to bother."

"O.K. I know how to make a swell tent," Terry said. "There's a big kid I know in town, lives next door. He makes a clothesline tent when it's hot."

"You won't tear Grandma's blankets?" Mother asked, a little anxiously. "Jim Jackson uses an old camp blanket to make his tent. It doesn't matter if he drives stakes through the corners."

"Oh." Terry puckered his forehead. He tried not to sound disappointed.

Briskly Grandma told Terry, "I have just the thing you need, Terry. Some rubber fruit-jar rings. I brought them, in case we found blackberries. Sew the rings to the corners of the blankets and drive stakes through the circles."

"Oh, boy, Grandma!" Terry agreed happily.

"Can't we girls sleep out, too?" Merry demanded.

"Me, too?" Penny asked.

Mother looked as if she was going to say No, then changed her mind. Penny was so often left out of Tucker adventures. "Of course," Mother said, "if Tina will share a tent with you."

"We'll have a girls' camp and a boys' camp," Tina planned.

"On opposite ends of the clothesline," Terry warned. "Girls giggle, don't they, Butch?"

Butch flushed to the roots of his white hair. "Uh, I don't know much about girls," he admitted. "I don't have a twin." He smiled shyly at Merry.

"But—" Penny began. She looked puzzled, then whispered to Tina, "I forgot Dutch was a make-believe twin."

Tom headed for the house, swinging his arms. His cheeks and ears were pink with the effort of planning and doing. "Let's get to work," Tom called.

Grandma handed out her most worn blankets.

Mother found the rubber jar rings. Tina brought darning needles from Grandma's big sewing basket.

Tom shared his big ball of twine. "Use all you need," he offered generously. "I can get more off the grocery packages."

Butch and Terry took a hatchet into the woods to cut long stakes. Toby followed. Merry raked the space under the clotheslines. Penny swept the ground and Sugar batted twigs.

Dad and Uncle Fred carried folding cots from the car in the parking lot.

Grandpa climbed to the shed attic. He handed down the folding cots he kept there for unexpected guests.

Merry, Tina, Penny, and Tom stood at the foot of the ladder. Each claimed a cot for his own bed.

"Just stack them," Grandpa said. "I'll carry them for you."

"We can carry our own!" Tina insisted as she carried her cot toward the house.

Tina and Merry carried their own beds. Tom tried, then had to accept help from Grandpa.

Penny trotted beside Uncle Fred. "Be careful, Uncle Fred," Penny warned. "Don't drop my bed!"

All the grownups carried their lawn chairs to the back yard. There they sat in the shade. They talked to each other and called suggestions to the tent-town builders.

Terry came out of the woods with Butch. He pointed at the space near the beach path. "Dibs!" he yelled.

The three girls arranged their cots by the kitchen door. Penny's bed was in the middle.

Tom refused to sleep between Terry and Butch. "I'm not a baby," he insisted, even though he was youngest of the group.

Merry lay down on her cot and stretched. She jiggled and wiggled. "Do I need a flat stone under a cot leg?" she asked Tina anxiously.

"They're all steady," Tina decided.

Merry gathered her blanket into a bundle on her cot. She bit her lips while she stitched one rubber ring into each corner of her blue blanket. When that was done she proudly showed her work to Mother.

"Pretty big stitches," Mother said. She tested them with her hands.

Merry grinned. "Big stitches are easy to pull out when Grandma needs her blanket."

Penny worked on one corner of her blanket while Tina and Merry sewed her remaining three rings in place. Once more Penny swept around her cot. Sugar jumped at the broom and swatted it.

Tom refused help. He did not know how to sew, but he made dozens of loops and tied knots. "Go 'way, Sugar," he ordered when the cat tangled his string.

They put a blanket over the line above each cot. Then Butch and Terry drove long wooden stakes through the rubber rings.

"There!" Terry said with much satisfaction when he pounded the last stake. Each little house was a different color. Each blanket was now a roof.

From sleeping porch and trailer, they carried sleeping bags and spread them on the cots. Butch had no sleeping bag, but Uncle Fred loaned his.

Merry jiggled on her toes. She looked at the sun, still high in the sky. "I hope dark comes early tonight," she sighed.

"Early!" Terry scoffed, but he knew what Merry meant. He, too, itched to crawl inside his own little house to sleep with the stars and night wind for company.

"See you later," Butch told Terry.

Puzzled, Tina watched Butch hurry down the beach. Why did he always head for the Arney house, when no Smiths lived on the north shore of Lake Annabelle?

While Tina watched Butch, Aunt Anne asked, "Do you think it is time to start a fire, Fred?"

"Good idea," Uncle Fred said. He went to the parking lot, Tom and Toby at his heels. He returned with a damp tow sack.

"Corn on the cob?" Tom asked. He trotted beside Uncle Fred and poked the lumps and bumps in the sack.

"Oh, boy, corn in a sand oven!" Terry shouted excitedly.

At the beach Father spaded a hole for the corn. Terry, Merry, and Tom gathered firewood. Uncle Fred dumped the unshucked corn on the sand. Tina and Penny arranged the corn in criss-cross rows in the hole Father had dug. Then Father scooped sand over the corn. He built a tiny fire on top of the food.

When the blaze had eaten into the twigs, Father added wood. Tom staggered down the beach with so much wood he could not see over the top. Toby ran in circles around him.

"O.K. Tom," Father agreed. "You may be fireman, and I'll be your helper."

With an arm around Toby, Tom squatted by the fire, ready to add wood. Father sat near to watch for flying sparks. The rest of the Tuckers hurried from the picnic table to the kitchen and back again.

Hungrily the Tuckers sniffed the air when Father uncovered the steaming corn.

From Grandpa to Tom, they ate so much buttered corn Father looked in one of Tom's ears to see if corn was coming out. "I like corn," Tom declared.

Night could not come fast enough for the younger Tuckers. When the last streak of sunset left the sky, Tom told everybody good night. He disappeared inside his red tent.

"That beats all," Grandpa said with a chuckle. "That's the first time I ever saw Tom go to bed willingly."

Just at dusk Butch hurried into the yard where the Tuckers watched the sunset on Lake Annabelle.

Terry greeted him joyously. "Hi, Butch! I thought you'd never get here."

Butch flushed. Shyly he told Mother, "My mom says thank you for inviting me."

"We're happy to have you here, Butch," Mother said warmly.

There was a hustle-bustle from bathroom to kitchen to trailer to the tent camp. Finally when every child was in bed, Father, Mother, Grandpa, Grandma, Uncle Fred, and Aunt Anne visited each blanket house to say good night.

When Father turned the flashlight inside Terry's tent, he whistled. "I hope you don't get hungry, son," he said politely.

Terry knew he was being teased, so he answered just as politely, "I'll try to make my supplies last." Beside his bed Terry had collected a plate of cookies, a glass of milk, two tuna fish sandwiches, half a cantaloupe and a spoon, a small box of raisins, a flashlight, and an old bent pie tin.

Father picked up the pie tin. "What's this for?"

Promptly Terry told him, "That's my alarm, of course."

When the adults left the yard, stillness filled all the space from earth to sky. Gradually sound returned. Tina could hear the friendly chirp of crickets. Night birds peeped. Waves slapped the dock. Inside the house, somebody laughed. Tina

sighed with pleasure. She called softly, "Are you O.K., Penny?"

"Isn't this fun?" Penny answered happily.

Suddenly Merry giggled.

"What's funny?" Terry called from the end of the line.

"I hid Sugar inside my sleeping bag and he tickles!" Merry squealed.

Toby walked along the line. He sniffed and made little woofy sounds. When Toby was sure he had located all the Tuckers, he curled up on the foot of Tom's cot. Tina could hear Toby snuffle as he chewed cheatgrass from his big woolly feet.

When nobody talked or giggled, Tina could hear the swish of wind in the trees. Grandpa's boat squeaked when it pulled on its mooring chain. Overhead a plane droned along the airway. Sleepily Tina wondered what it was like, flying through the night.

Just as she dozed, she heard Mother and Father cross the yard to the vacation trailer. Knowing they were near made her feel warm and safe.

Suddenly Tina wakened. She knew she had slept, but she had no idea what time it was. The sky looked like a big black sieve turned over the world, with a million stars shining through its holes.

But what was that sound?

Tina strained to listen. It wasn't Toby moving around. Toby was big, but his feet did not thump the ground. She named each sound she heard. Owl. Wind. Waves.

And that other sound. Shuffle. Wheeze. *Thunk.*

"Oh!"

Something bumped Tina's blanket roof. Something breathed.

Tina sat up straight in bed. She reached for her flashlight.

"T-Tina!" Penny's voice was a shivery little whisper in the dark.

"What's the matter, honey?" Tina asked anxiously.

"There's something out there, isn't there?"

"I—I think so," Tina said honestly. "Do you want me to sleep with you?"

"Oh, would you?" Penny begged.

Silently Tina crept from her bed to Penny's. A shadow moved toward the beach path. It was bigger and blacker than the shadows cast in the starlight by the house and trees. Tina's heart thumped with relief when she snuggled down beside Penny.

"Maybe it will go away if we don't make any noise," Penny whispered.

"I'm sure it will," Tina told Penny. She hoped she calmed Penny. She certainly did not convince herself. Something was out there. Something big.

Tina's imagination filled the night with bears, wolves, and bobcats, though no large wild animals had been seen near the cottage for years. That shadow was bigger than any wild animal she could think of. It was as big as a cow—but it couldn't be a cow. She had visited Uncle Fred's dairy farm often enough to know the sounds a cow made. Tina was sure that black blob of shadow was not a cow.

Penny made little choking sounds. Then she coughed. "I'm s-sorry," she told Tina. "I can't h-help it. I have to cough." The more Penny tried to choke back the gasping sounds in her throat, the louder she coughed.

"Sit up," Tina said. "Maybe you can breathe better that way."

Penny tried, but still she coughed.

Tina heard restless movements in the other tents.

"Sst!" Terry hissed. "Is Penny sick?"

When Terry spoke, Tina heard a little nickering sound near Butch's tent. Then a branch snapped.

"What's going *glup-snuff?*" Merry asked in a tense half-whisper.

"I don't know," Tina whispered back.

"I want M-Mother!" Penny wailed between coughs.

Tina's heart rose in her throat. How could she cross that space between the clothesline and the trailer? Penny coughed again. Sympathy for Penny overcame Tina's fear. "Come on," she said. "I'll take you to the trailer."

"I'll go with you," Merry offered.

"So will I," Terry called.

Four of the five Tuckers crept from the tent

camp to the trailer. They walked so carefully their toes dug into the ground.

"We're leaving Tom!" tenderhearted Penny wailed.

"We'll go right back," Terry promised. He swung his flashlight in a circle. "See? There's nothing by Tom's tent, and Toby is with him."

Tina knew Terry would give his eyeteeth to go in the trailer and shut the door. So would she, but Tom could not be left alone.

The trailer door stood open. Quickly Penny climbed the ladder to her bunk. "I'm all right now," she whispered. "If I cough, Mother will wake up."

Tina wanted to shake Father awake. But how silly she would feel to arouse the family and find nothing in the yard. "I'm no coward!" she told herself. She tried to believe it.

As silently as cats, Tina, Merry, and Terry crossed the yard again. Tina thought she saw bushes move near the path to the beach. "Let's all aim our flashlights at the path," she whispered.

Three lights were bigger than one. Still they saw nothing.

"We might as well go to bed," Merry said sensibly. "We'll light the path for you, Terry."

"I don't want girls to take care of me," Terry objected.

"Don't be silly," Merry told him. "There are two of us and just one of you. Besides, I'm going to sleep in Penny's tent. With my head so close to Tina's feet, I can get in bed with her if I get scared."

Merry and Tina stood close together while they held their lights for Terry. Suddenly he started walking backward, very slowly.

"What's wrong?" Merry cried.

"Ssh!" Terry hissed. "There's a skunk in my tent. He's eating my food!"

"Maybe we can scare him with our lights," Merry suggested. "Aren't animals afraid of light?"

"Not skunks," Terry informed her earnestly. "They're not afraid of anything!"

Standing well away from Terry's tent, the girls spotlighted the animal.

"Isn't it pretty?" Merry whispered.

"Pretty stinky if it gets mad at us," Terry warned.

Waving its big tail, the black and white skunk pushed and nosed Terry's hoard of food. The skunk ate Terry's tuna fish, then marched down the beach path.

"And I didn't even get to beat my tin plate!" Terry moaned.

Finally the Tuckers returned to their beds, but Tina did not sleep. She could hear the twins move restlessly. She knew they were awake, too. Almost at once, after the skunk left, the strange whickery, thumping, snuffling sounds began again.

Tina scooted down in her sleeping bag till her head was covered. She tried not to hear the mysterious sounds.

But she heard them! *Whiffle. Snuff. Clump.*

What was out there in the dark?

6
Terry's Trick

Tina awoke with a start and remembered her fright in the night. She listened. Cheerful little sounds came from the sleeping porch and the trailer. That meant Uncle Fred and Aunt Anne, Mother and Father were awake. Tina crawled to the foot of her cot and stuck her head through the V opening. Now that sunshine lighted the back yard, she felt embarrassed about having been so scared.

Grandpa stepped through the kitchen door. He stretched in the sun. He rubbed his bushy white hair. Grandma joined him. She tied on a big white apron.

"Who left the gate open?" Grandpa rumbled.

"There's a horse in the yard!"

Tina gasped.

A horse! She had been afraid of a *horse.*

She jiggled the head of Penny's cot where Merry had finished the night. Instantly Merry's head popped up. "Is our monster back?" Merry demanded.

"It was a horse," Tina confessed. "Grandpa said so."

"A horse!" Merry's eyes widened. Then she put her hands over her mouth to hold back a giggle. "Does Terry know?"

"Not unless he's awake."

"Then let's wake him," Merry said promptly. She jumped out of bed and told Tina, "Put your clothes on, quick!"

In sunsuits and sneakers, Tina and Merry ran across the yard. Terry slept with both arms flung above his curly dark head. Tom lay on top of his sleeping bag. Butch had his head covered.

Merry's dark eyes sparkled with mischief. She drew Tina behind a bush and cupped her hands over her mouth. She made whiffling, blowing noises.

Terry's hands jerked and he sat up. Tina and Merry saw him reach for his pie tin and flashlight. Then he began to beat a noisy alarm. *Whing! Whang! Whum!*

Tom rolled out of bed and crawled through the side of his tent instead of the end. His eyes were so wide open they looked painted on his face. Tom's head turned while he examined the whole side of the yard facing the lake. Then he scrambled towards Terry's tent on his hands and knees. Toby waggled along behind Tom, sniffing at Tom's bare feet. He dog-laughed with interest in Tom's odd behavior.

"Be careful, Tom!" Terry warned. "Duck out of sight until I scare it away." Again Terry beat the tin pan. *Whang! Wham!*

Butch pawed out of his sleeping bag. He looked like a turtle popping its head out of its shell.

"It?" Butch repeated sleepily. "What's it?"

"Some animal," Terry said in a loud whisper. "It hung around all night."

Behind their bush, Tina and Merry were close enough to touch the excited boys. They could see every movement the boys made.

When Tom reached Terry's tent he stood up and looked around. "I don't see anything to get so 'cited about!" he said.

"You should have been awake last night, Tom," Terry said earnestly. He peered around, ready to beat another alarm. "There was a skunk in my tent."

"Honest?" Butch asked.

"Yeah, and he ate my tuna fish," Terry complained. "And there was this other animal. A big one! It was here all night!" His eyes widened as he measured a large space between his hands.

Tom did not look convinced. "Then why didn't Toby chase it away?" he asked.

"Guess he's too smart to chase a skunk," Butch said. "Some dogs are."

"I mean, why didn't he chase the big 'un away?" Tom asked patiently.

Neither Terry nor Butch had an answer. Both taller boys walked barefoot around their tents. Terry looked at the bushes and the corners of the house and shed, but Butch studied the ground.

Behind the bush Tina nudged Merry. Tina

stood up carefully to see what Butch was doing.

Butch squatted on his heels and ran his fingers around a horse's hoofprint. Butch grinned, then bit his lips. With a blank look on his face he stood up and faced Terry. "What do you think hung around all night?" Butch asked.

Terry ran his fingers through his dark, curly hair. His blue eyes were wide. Wisely he nodded his head and told Butch, "Must have been a bear. It was big. Probably it was after my food."

Merry held her nose to keep from giggling. Then she blew through her hands again. Both Merry and Tina peeped to see what happened.

Terry carried his heavy flashlight in one hand like a club. In the other he held the tin plate. He bent from the waist and started a stealthy retreat to the kitchen. He was closely followed by Tom, who stopped every few steps to look around the yard. Tom did not look frightened. He looked puzzled.

Butch walked straight to the bushes which lined the beach path. He led an old brown horse into the open yard.

"Is this the bear you heard?" Butch asked

Terry, just as Terry passed the last clothesline tent.

"Wh-What—" Terry gasped.

For the first time since the Tuckers had known him, Butch burst out laughing. He laughed so hard he rolled on the grass. "A h-horse!" Butch gasped. "You were afraid of a horse!"

Terry frowned, then looked sheepish. "Guess I was," he admitted. Suspiciously he asked Butch, "But how did you know there was a horse in the yard?"

Butch pointed at the ground. "I saw hoof marks," he said.

"I knew Toby didn't smell a bear," Tom told Terry. "Toby wouldn't let us sleep while a bear was here."

Hotly Terry demanded, "Well, why didn't he bark at a horse?"

"Who's scared of a horse?" Tom asked, and he went into the kitchen.

Stiffly Terry walked back to his tent. "Gotta get dressed," he said shortly.

"Ooh," Merry whispered behind her hand to Tina. "We'd better get out of here fast. Terry is going to get even with somebody."

"We shouldn't have teased him," Tina said. "Remember, we were scared, too."

Merry shrugged, then giggled.

Tina followed Merry to the kitchen for breakfast, but her mind was not on food. It was on Tom's question, "Who's afraid of a horse?" Of course Toby was not afraid of a horse. But why didn't Toby bark?

Breakfast was served around the big table in the kitchen. Grandma mixed a big bowl of batter till it was foamy with egg whites. Aunt Anne fried pancakes on one griddle. Mother used the other. The hotcakes they made seemed to melt from plates. Every bite of Aunt Anne's country butter and maple syrup was eaten.

Terry ate six pancakes with an egg and crisp bacon. All around him Tuckers made cheerful plans for the day. Terry did not join the table talk. He kept his eyes fixed on the far horizon where the Blue River drained Lake Annabelle. Once in the while he glanced at Butch.

Merry, too, looked at Butch. The new boy was not quite so colorless as he had been the first time she saw him. Now his white skin was tanned. His pale hair, lashes, and brows looked pasted on. She was glad Butch had nice table manners. Mother and Grandma were particular about that.

Only Tom chattered about spending the night in the yard, and he had slept through the excitement.

Father asked politely, "How's your appetite this morning, Terry?" He winked at Uncle Fred.

"Yes, Terry," Uncle Fred teased, "did your supplies hold out?"

Terry told about the skunk in his tent. Tina explained why Penny was taken back to the trailer. But nobody mentioned the horse.

Thoughtfully Merry studied Terry's face. When Terry was quiet, something was about to happen.

When breakfast was finished, Butch said thank you to Mother and Grandma. He asked them to tell him when an hour had passed. "That's when I have to go home," he explained.

"I have a watch," Merry told Butch. "I'll remind you."

Aunt Anne and Uncle Fred said they must go home right after lunch, so Butch returned Uncle Fred's sleeping bag. Then Butch helped Tina and Merry take down the tents. Penny snipped threads with her small scissors. Tom pulled the rubber rings off the corners of Grandma's blankets. Father and Uncle Fred rolled sleeping bags and folded cots.

Terry did not help. He disappeared.

Several times Merry and Tina raised their eyebrows at each other. They looked at the lake.

"Oh, Terry is all right," Merry said. "He has too much sense to go swimming for an hour after eating." Just the same, she wondered where Terry was and what he was doing.

In the bustle of pushing chairs into place after breakfast, Terry had left the kitchen. He ran across the back yard and ducked into the shed hooked onto the garage. A chest stood in one corner. Terry knew just what he was looking for. Quickly he found both his and Tom's baseball mitts. Terry put on one of the mitts. He thumped his left hand into the palm. Yep! These mitts were exactly right for what he had in mind. He thought for a minute and looked around.

Terry hunted for Tom's stilts. They were not in plain sight, so he climbed the ladder and searched the attic. No stilts. Then he remembered having seen the stilts on the beach.

Keeping out of sight of the house, Terry ran toward the beach. There he fastened the ball mitts to the bottoms of Tom's stilts. He walked a few steps in the sand. He looked back at the tracks he made.

"Boy!" he grunted. "I'll just see if old Butch knows what made *these* tracks!"

Terry walked in a wobbling line down the beach. Sometimes he walked in the fine white sand and sometimes he walked in wet sand where the waves slip-slapped. He came to a tiny brook that ran into Lake Annabelle from a spring. There Terry punched deep tracks like those left by a huge animal at a waterhole.

Then Terry wandered off into the woods, crossed a rocky space and hid the stilts. He walked back, being careful to leave no footprints near the big, blobby tracks he had made.

Terry grinned. Those tracks looked real enough to fool anybody. "Now I'll just call Butch," he muttered. "It's my turn to laugh."

In the bushes at the edge of the yard, Terry hid to see what Butch was doing. He could hear Mother, Grandma, and Aunt Anne working in the kitchen. In the parking lot Father, Uncle Fred, and Grandpa kicked Uncle Fred's tires. They walked around his car. Merry and Tina folded Grandma's blankets in the back yard. Penny swept up scraps of string. Tom played ring-toss with Grandma's jar rubbers. He used one of the tent stakes for a goal.

Terry pulled his brows together. Where was Butch, anyway?

Leaves moved. Twigs snapped.

Terry jumped with surprise, then sank behind his bush again. Puzzled, he watched Butch lead the old brown horse down the beach path and into the woods. Once Butch stopped to scratch the horse's nose and pat a shoulder. The horse followed willingly.

In a few minutes Butch returned to the back yard. His face was very red, as if he had been running. Tom gave Butch some rubber rings. He threw one at the wooden stake.

Just as Butch balanced to toss another ring, Terry burst out of the bushes.

"The rickermeracker!" Terry screamed. "The rickermeracker is in the woods!"

7
Blondy and Muscle Man

"The rickermeracker," Terry panted. "I c-came through the b-bushes so he wouldn't see me—but I saw you on the path, Butch—and I had to warn you. *Don't* go down the beach path. The *rickermeracker* is in the woods!"

In the sunshine of the back yard Merry and Tina moved closer together. They put their arms around Penny and Tom. They had never heard of a rickermeracker. But there were lots of things in the world they had never heard about. What had Terry seen?

"Will it bite?" Penny asked anxiously.

Merry saw Terry hesitate when Penny cried out. She kicked Tina's ankle just hard enough to make Tina turn her head. "It's a trick," she whispered.

Quickly Terry told Penny, "The rickermeracker doesn't bother girls. Just boys. And horses!"

"W-Well," Penny said hesitantly. "Are you sure?"

"I'm sure!" Terry raised his hand in Scout's Honor.

Butch's pale eyelashes flickered. "Wh-which way did it go?" he asked.

Terry widened his eyes. "You mean, the horse?"

"No. The ricker— the what-you-said." Butch clenched his hands into fists. He stretched tall to look down the spring path.

"The rickermeracker?" Terry asked, sounding breathless. "He went that-away!" The tip of Terry's finger aimed straight at the spot in the woods where he had seen Butch hide the old brown horse.

Butch did not ask another question. He started down the path.

Terry picked up a dry twig and broke it.

Butch jumped. He stopped walking. He looked and listened.

Tina, Merry, Tom, and Penny followed Terry. Terry scowled fiercely and put his finger on his lips. "Ssh," he whispered. "Go back!"

Tina reached for Tom's and Penny's hands, but Merry followed. "You said the rickermeracker doesn't hurt girls," she reminded Terry. "But it *might* hurt boys, so I'm going along to scare it away from *you*."

Terry's scowl changed to a grin. He winked at Merry. Loudly he explained to Butch, "I found its tracks on the beach. Want to see them? You might never see another rickermeracker's tracks in your whole life. Almost nobody ever sees a rickermeracker!"

"But the horse," Butch worried. "You said it hurts horses."

Terry seemed to consider Butch's words. With a straight face he outlined a plan. "Let's follow the rickermeracker's tracks. If we know where he is, we will know if the horse is in danger."

"Uh, O.K.," Butch agreed, with another anxious glance at the bushes.

Terry pushed through the bushes between the yard and the sandy beach. He made a great deal of noise. "To scare away the rickermeracker," he told Butch.

Butch, too, made all the noise he could.

Tingling with curiosity, Merry followed the boys. By this time she was sure the trick was directed at Butch. But she was a little wary. Terry's tricks did not always turn out the way he planned them.

When they reached the beach, Terry pointed at the first track. "See? It must have jumped out of the bushes."

"W-Wow!" Butch gasped. "It's a big 'un, isn't it?" Butch put his foot in one of the tracks. His foot was big, but the rickermeracker's was huge. Merry stared at the size of the tracks. She felt a shiver run down her spine. Maybe Terry *had* seen a rickermeracker, after all. The only footprints in the sand were the new ones they were making right this minute.

Intently Merry studied the sand, then looked at the bushes. No branches were broken. Nothing had come through the undergrowth.

Terry waved his arms. "The rickermeracker is tall," he explained.

"How do you know?" Merry asked suspiciously.

"He has to be," Terry argued. "See? He stepped right over the bushes and he waded out into the lake."

Butch dropped to his knees and examined the big, blobby track.

Merry knelt beside Butch. She peeped up through her lashes to study Terry's face. Terry looked much too innocent not to be guilty of something. Why had she allowed herself to be worried, even for a minute? Terry's jeans had creases to show they had been rolled. And one leg was damp. That rickermeracker had waded, all right!

Butch's lips trembled when he said, "He must be as big as an elephant."

"Oh, bigger," Terry agreed with a straight face.

Merry squirmed with curiosity. How on earth had Terry made those tracks? "That old rickermeracker doesn't weigh very much," Merry told

Butch. "Look. Those tracks aren't very deep."

"I found some deep ones. Come on, I'll show you!" Terry jumped up. He pointed at the tracks which crossed the beach, entered the water, and wandered into the edge of the woods.

At the spring Butch studied the tracks with real worry. "Hadn't we better go back?" he asked.

Terry shrugged. "Oh, I don't think so. A rickermeracker sleeps when he is full of water. Anybody can see he had a good drink at the spring."

"But the horse," Butch said uneasily. He studied the tracks again. He looked undecided. "What *is* a rickermeracker anyway? I never heard of one. What does he eat?"

"I told you, he eats—" Terry began.

At just that moment there was a popping sound. A flock of birds flew out of the trees around the spring. Merry, Terry, and Butch became silent while they tried to locate the cause of the disturbance.

"Was that the r-rickermeracker?" Butch asked in alarm.

Merry scowled at Terry to let him know she thought his joke had gone far enough. "Sounded to me like a gunshot," she said, so positively Terry could not build his tall tale any higher.

"I thought so, too," Terry agreed.

The underbrush crackled. Butch stepped between Merry and the danger spot.

Merry whispered fiercely, "Terry, you ought to be ashamed of yourself for scaring Butch. He isn't going to let *me* get hurt. That's more than I can say for some people I know."

Terry reddened. He *was* standing behind Merry, while Butch guarded her. "O.K.," he muttered. "I'll tell him."

Before Terry could explain about the rickermeracker tracks, two tall boys pushed through the bushes.

One was thin and blond, with a lot of curly hair and a bony, sunburned face. The other boy looked older. He had a shadow of mustache on his upper lip, bold black eyes, and a strong, muscular body. He carried a twenty-two rifle.

"Blondy and Muscle Man," Terry muttered close to Merry's right ear.

"What are you punks doin' out here in the woods?" Muscle Man demanded. The words began in a deep growl, but ended in a broken squeak. The teen-age boy moved his shoulders with embarrassment. He motioned with his gun. "Get outa the path and let a couple of men go by," he ordered.

Merry resented both manner and words. She widened her eyes and asked, "Where are the men?"

"Why, you—" Muscle Man stepped forward, but Blondy held him back. "Take it easy," Blondy said, a little nervously. "This little kid's old man may be around. Ever think of that?"

Terry placed himself ahead of Butch. He stuck out his chin. "You can't order my sister around!" Terry declared. He glanced at Butch to draw courage from the other boy's presence. To Terry's surprise, Butch was no longer standing beside him. Terry felt very lonely and small, facing the two tall boys. He made fists to hold onto his own courage.

Muscle Man shrugged as if he had lost interest in anybody under twenty-one. He poked out his lips in a lopsided grin. "Big stuff," he sneered. His black eyes glittered at Merry and Terry. But he looked longest at Butch who had moved down the path.

"Hey!" Blondy said excitedly. He nudged Muscle Man. "There's a kingfisher. Think you can get him?"

"Sure. Easy." Muscle Man raised his gun and squinted.

Merry, too, heard the kingfisher's hunting cry. She discovered it on a bare limb over the spring. One quick glance told her no person was in the line of fire. Only the kingfisher was in danger.

"You can't shoot birds!" Terry argued. He started toward Muscle Man, but Merry kicked his ankle. Terry stopped in his tracks.

"Just watch me," Muscle Man retorted.

Muscle Man squinted along the barrel of his twenty-two.

As a violinist, Merry was used to waiting for an exact time to move. She watched Muscle Man's fingers as intently as if he directed an orchestra. Then, just as his finger squeezed the trigger, Merry yelled. His finger jerked and the shot went wild. When the bullet exploded, the kingfisher flew away. His rattling, noisy cry warned every bird in the woods of danger.

Angrily Muscle Man turned on Merry.

Terry thought fast. In any sort of struggle Muscle Man and Blondy were winners before they started. But from the careless way Muscle Man handled that gun, Terry was sure the tall boys were not used to the woods.

"The rickermeracker!" Terry yelled. "It's behind you!"

Both tall boys jerked their heads to look over their shoulders.

Merry and Terry darted back down the path they had followed.

"If you don't believe me," Terry shouted back, "look at the tracks around the spring!"

Merry ran as fast as she could. She did not rest until she reached the open beach. There she dropped in a heap on the sand. Terry tumbled down beside her.

"Where's Butch?" Merry asked with alarm.

"He jumped into the bushes wh-when the g-gun went off," Terry panted.

The twins listened for the pounding of feet on the path. When the tall boys did not appear, Merry relaxed. She sifted a handful of sand onto her legs and watched it slide off.

But Terry did not relax. He sat up straight and stared at the spot in the bushes where Butch had disappeared. That was near the place he had seen Butch hide the old brown horse before breakfast.

"Very funny," he muttered.

"Funny ha-ha, or funny queer?" Merry wanted to know.

Terry wrinkled his dark brows. "Funny queer," he said. He told Merry what he had seen, then asked, "Why was Butch so worried about that old horse? That must have been the reason he ducked."

"I don't know, but he was brave about the rickermeracker," Merry reminded him, remembering the way Butch had shielded her.

"He was scared of those boys," Terry said with dignity.

"So were we," Merry insisted.

"Yeah," Terry muttered. "But I think Butch

had seen those boys before."

Merry shrugged and tossed back her dark hair. "So what?" she asked pertly. "Terry Tucker, how did you make those rickermeracker tracks?"

"Wouldn't you like to know?" Terry teased.

8
A Trespasser

An hour later the five Tuckers boarded the Tub for their daily boat trip to collect milk cartons. Grandpa laid an extra oar across the seats. "That's your spare tire in case you have a flat," he said with a chuckle.

Father set a gallon can under the bow. "Here's some extra gas in case you run out," he said.

"Thanks, Father," Merry said with a wide grin. "But I checked our gas. I'm pilot today."

While Grandpa and Father watched from the dock, Merry guided the Tub to open water. She waved gaily. Then she tossed her head to let the wind push her hair. She felt a tingle of excitement. She imagined herself headed for distant shores and high adventure.

When they could no longer see Father and Grandpa, Terry leaned back in the bow seat. He braced his feet on the center seat where Tina sat between Penny and Tom. "It's about time we look for that oar we lost," Terry declared.

"We've watched for that oar ever since we lost it," Merry reminded him. "Where there's so much water and shore, how can we figure out where to hunt?"

Tina turned to face Merry in the stern of the Tub. "We might go back to the spot where we lost the oar," Tina planned. "When the boat drifts, we can tell which direction the current flows and head for that shore."

"Oh, sure," Merry said pertly. "We'll count the waves till we find number ninety-nine. That's where we lost the oar."

"I'll count," Penny offered. "One—, two—"

Tina hugged Penny. "Merry's making a joke."

"Sure she is. Nobody can count waves," Tom declared wisely. He looked accusingly at Tina. "And nobody can go back to a spot on water without a compass. Grandpa says so."

"That's right," Tina agreed with Tom. "But if we can remember what we saw on shore, we can go back to almost the same spot."

"We picked up Butch near the bathhouse," Merry said at once.

Terry agreed with Merry and added, "I headed straight out from a bunch of birch trees west of the boathouse."

Tina looked through her lashes while she recalled the way the oar had slid over each wave before she could touch it. "The closest beach was the one where the wild rice grows," she said. Then she exclaimed, "That's it!"

"Where?" Tom asked. "Where do you see the oar?"

Tina wrinkled her nose at her small brother. "I don't see the oar, Tom, but I almost know where it went. The oar moved over the waves *away* from the woods where we found the shack. Every time I turned my head to breathe, I saw something red."

"Red?" Merry repeated.

"It would have to be something big to be seen from the middle of the bay," Terry said. "Maybe it was a boat near the shore."

"It didn't move," Tina insisted.

"Maybe the boat was tied to a dock," Tom said practically. "Or was upside down on sand."

"Maybe," Tina admitted, "but I think the red spot was bigger than a boat."

"That beats all," Terry said, puzzled.

"Let's go get our cartons," Merry said. She headed for the cottage colony on the north shore.

"O.K.," Terry agreed. "We can keep our eyes open while we ride."

By the time the last carton was collected for the day, nothing large and red had been seen. When they returned to the Tub. Terry said, "Maybe it would help us to remember if we sit where we sat when we lost the oar."

"But it's my turn to steer today," Merry objected noisily. Then curiosity about the lost oar and the red spot overcame her wish to keep her turn. "O.K.," she told Terry. "You may be pilot."

They cruised around and around the bay. But they could not agree on the spot where they had lost Grandpa's oar.

When they were almost ready to give up, Tina shaded her eyes. "I see it." she declared excitedly. "I see something red!"

Carefully Terry placed the Tub in line with the shore as he remembered it. Then he turned off the motor and set the Tub adrift.

"This'll take time," Terry said. He folded his arms and slid down on his spine.

Penny put the palms of her hands together. "Let's play What Am I?" she suggested eagerly.

"It!" Tom said promptly. He frowned at Terry. "No fair asking questions I can't answer," he warned.

"O.K.," Terry agreed. "We'll ask easy questions."

What Am I? was a favorite game used by the Tuckers to while away time. From the lazy way the Tub rocked on the current, there would be time enough for a dozen games before the boat reached shore.

"What am I?" Tom demanded. His eyes were wide and blue with the excitement of being It.

Terry thought of the horse he had seen Butch hide. "Do you eat grass?" he asked Tom.

Tom giggled. "No, I don't eat cheatgrass," he said.

Merry thought of Sugar. "Are you black and white?" she asked.

"No, I'm not a skunk," Tom answered promptly.

Penny thought of her paper dolls. "Do you put on clothes?" she asked.

"Yes, I put on shoes," Tom said.

From the way Tom sneaked a glance at his own shoes, Tina knew Penny's question was "hot." "Are you a boy?" she asked.

"Yes!" Tom shouted and laughed. "I'm Tom!"

"Hey!" Terry said admiringly. "That's a good one. I would never have thought of myself."

Penny waved her hand. "It!" she said.

Terry thought of the blanket tents they had set up on the clothesline last night. "Do you cover something?" he asked.

"That's a hard question," Penny objected. She whispered to Merry, "What's another word for 'cover'?"

"Hide," Merry whispered back.

Aloud Penny told Terry, "No, I don't hide

heads." She waited for the next question.

Tina thought of Aunt Anne's picnic. "Are you good to eat?" she asked.

"No, I'm not candy!" Penny declared.

Tom thought of the milk cartons. "Do you hold something?" he asked.

Penny stared at the water for a long time before she answered. "Yes, I hold seats," she agreed.

"Are you a car?" Merry asked, thinking of the Tuckers' old blue station wagon.

"No, I'm not a car," Penny retorted quickly.

"Are you a chair?" Terry asked.

"No, I'm not Grandma's rocking chair," Penny said. Her blue eyes sparkled with the fun of outwitting Terry.

"You're not a car and you're not a chair," Tina mused. "But you have seats. Oh! Are you a boat?"

"Yes, I am the Tub!" Penny giggled so hard she slid off the center seat and sat on the floorboards of the boat.

Merry had been standing on her knees. Her crossed arms resting on the bow made a pillow for her head while the Tub rocked on the current. Suddenly she sat up straight. "There's our red spot," she said excitedly.

"The Arney house, of course," Tina agreed. She recognized the red fences and latticework around the white house as soon as Merry spoke.

"Shall I start the motor and head for shore?" Terry asked. "We're drifting toward the Arney beach."

"Let's," Tina urged.

As they came near the beach, Tina turned to ask Terry, "Have the Arneys been here?"

"Not since last August," Terry answered. "They live in Chicago. They can't run out for week ends."

"Well, somebody has been here," Tina declared. "Their boat is at the dock."

Terry altered his course slightly for a clear view of the Arney beach. There was no mistaking the red boat which was tied up at the dock. The name Arney was painted in white letters on its side.

"Maybe somebody has rented their cottage," Merry suggested.

"No," Terry said flatly.

"Why not?" Merry argued. "Lots of people rent cottages."

"I heard Mr. Arney tell Grandpa that he lives too far away to keep track of renters," Terry declared.

"Let's go ashore and look around," Tina suggested soberly. "If something is wrong, Grandpa can phone Mr. Arney."

On shore the Tuckers found both barefoot and shoe-prints on the sand. Bushes were broken along the paths.

"Somebody has been here!" Merry declared.

Terry knew where the boat was stored when not in use. He ran to the front of the house, where latticework made a room under the high front porch. The lock was broken on the double doors opposite the porch steps. Terry tightened his lips. "They didn't use a key to get the boat out," Terry called to Tina, who was shading her eyes to look through windows.

"Somebody has raised the window shades," Tina said. "I can see a lot of cans and food boxes on the kitchen table."

S M T W T F S
MILK
CORN
FLAKES
BEANS

"Mrs. Arney would never leave a messy kitchen," Merry insisted. "She's as neat as Grandma!"

The Tuckers gathered in a worried group. Each was afraid to say what he was thinking. It was Terry who spoke. "Betcha there's a trespasser," he said.

"What's a trespasser?" Tom asked. Anxiously he peered into the storage room under the front porch. "Will it bite us?"

"A trespasser is somebody who sneaks around where he isn't supposed to be," Tina explained.

Tom nodded his head wisely. "Then there's a trespasser," he said. "Here's his bait can." Tom picked up a pork and beans can. It was filled with black earth and wiggling, live worms.

Terry looked at Tina over the top of Tom's head. "We'd better get out of here," he warned. "Those worms haven't been out of the ground very long."

Quickly and silently the five Tuckers returned to the beach.

"Aren't we going to hunt for Grandpa's oar?" Tom asked.

Tina studied the twins' faces for the answer. Both shook their heads. "No, Tom," Tina answered. "We'll hunt for the oar some other day. We have found enough for one day."

Penny looked puzzled. "What did we find?" she asked.

"Trespasser tracks," Tom told her solemnly.

By the time the milk cartons were cleaned and stacked, Grandma called the Tuckers to lunch. They sat around the beach table where they could look at the lake while they ate.

Uncle Fred finished his second cup of coffee and stood up. "Time to travel," he said.

Aunt Anne looked alarmed. "It can't be time to leave, Fred."

"There's never enough time to spend with the people we love," Grandma said softly.

The whole family helped to repack the car. They found a dozen excuses to stay close together.

Finally Uncle Fred looked at his watch. "One o'clock," he stated. "Right, Merry?"

Merry looked at her small, heart-shaped watch. "Right," she agreed.

Each Tucker was hugged and invited to visit

the farm. Grandpa helped Aunt Anne into the car, and Uncle Fred started the motor. Aunt Anne thought of something she simply had to ask Grandma. But Uncle Fred said, "Write her a letter, Annie. Traffic is going to be busier than an ant hill, and we have a long way to go."

Noisy good-bys were shouted till Uncle Fred's car disappeared around the curve behind the parking lot. Then everybody stood and looked at each other. Suddenly something bright and happy was missing.

Mother asked, with a little tremble in her voice, "What do people do who have no family?"

Tina did not know the answer to Mother's question. Being a Tucker with brothers and sisters, mother and father, grandparents and uncles and aunts was a warm and wonderful thing.

"I wonder what Aunt Anne forgot?" Terry asked.

"She forgot to let us know if they are coming for the Fourth of July," Grandma said wisely.

Merry traded secret glances with Terry and Tina. The Fourth of July! Soon they would be

able to share their milk-carton secret. But was it possible that school had been out almost a month? That meant one third of vacation was gone.

"We're wasting time!" Terry shouted.

"You took the words right out of my mouth!" Merry agreed.

Pell-mell the five Tuckers ran through the back yard and down the beach path. As they passed the clotheslines, each grabbed his own big towel. They spread their towels in a favorite spot where some willows leaned toward Lake Annabelle. There the sand was always cool.

Branches spread a green roof like a tepee. The big soft towels looked like rugs.

Tom fell asleep the minute he shut his eyes. Penny wiggled on her white towel printed with yellow daisies. She, too, soon slept. But the three older Tuckers lay on their stomachs. They rested chins on folded hands. Drowsily they looked across the sand to the bouncing sun-sparkles on the water.

"If you know just where to look, you can see the Arney house," Terry said.

Tina located the house. But Merry put her face close to Terry's and squinted through her long, dark lashes. Finally she found the tiny red spot Terry said was the Arney house.

"I wonder who is living there," Tina worried.

"I wonder where Butch lives," Merry said.

"Me, too," Terry said, biting his lower lip. "Did you ever notice which way he goes when he leaves the beach?"

"He goes toward the Arney house," Merry declared. She felt a little scared to hear herself say the words she had been thinking.

Tina recalled a day she had sailed with Grandpa, Terry, and Butch. "Butch was worried when I saw something move at the Arney house," Tina said soberly.

"I've asked Dad, Grandpa, and Mr. Wilson. I've looked at names on boat docks and mail-boxes," Terry explained. "Nobody named Smith lives close enough for Butch to visit us, unless he has a boat."

"We all know Butch is afraid of boats," Tina added quickly.

"I think he rides that horse," Terry said thoughtfully. "The horse seemed to know him. Butch wasn't afraid of it."

"The Arney house has a stable," Merry re-membered.

Terry kicked Merry's ankle with his bare foot. He said, "Don't be silly. You know the Arneys didn't leave a horse to take care of itself all winter. Besides, they have good horses, not old nags."

"That isn't what I meant," Merry said, re-turning Terry's kick with spirit. "I'm just say-ing there is a place to keep a horse at the Arney house, if you happen to have a horse."

"And if you happen to need a place to keep a horse," Terry teased. "What time is it?"

Merry scrambled up. She tapped the face of her wrist watch. "Time's up. Let's go swimming."

Down the path Merry raced, followed by her brothers and sisters, all whooping like Indians.

Merry was just learning the running dive. Off the end of the dock she skimmed in a shallow dive. She came up swinging her arms in a crawl.

Tina saw a flash on one of Merry's brown arms. "Merry!" she shrieked. "You forgot to take off your watch!"

Merry let her feet drop. She walked water while she asked Tina to repeat what she had said. Her face puckered with dismay when she saw her precious watch drip water. "Oh!" Merry wailed. "What'll I do?" Hastily she swam back to the dock and climbed the ladder.

Terry tried to pull the watch off Merry's wrist before she was out of the water. "Let's take it to Father. He can open it up and dry it out," Terry said with a rush of words. When Merry was upset, so was Terry.

Merry saw Terry's puckered face and burst out laughing. "Father won't beat me, Terry," she said in a coaxing tone.

"Well, no," Terry agreed, grinning back at his twin. "But how will we know what time it is when we're on the beach? You had the only watch that ran."

Tom had been listening with a sober look on his face. "We need an alarm clock," he declared.

Terry looked at Tom with respect. "That would do it," he agreed. "But where will we find an alarm clock?"

"We have lots of them in the store," Penny

said, trying to be helpful.

"But they are on a counter in Yorkville, and we're at the lake, remember?" Terry reminded.

Father and Grandpa ambled across the dock and spread big shadows over the Tuckers huddled around Merry.

"Having trouble?" Father asked.

Terry gave him Merry's watch. Merry said, "I'm sorry."

"You aren't the first Tucker to swim with a watch on," Father said, waggling his eyebrows at Grandpa. "I've dunked a few watches myself."

Grandpa grinned in the special way that made the Tuckers remember Father had not always been a grownup. Not too very long ago Father had been the boy on the beach, and Grandpa had been a father, not a grandfather.

"Tom thinks we need an alarm clock," Terry said.

Grandpa nodded his head till his white hair waved. "That's a good idea, Tom. But what about a sundial? You can build one on the sand with a handful of sticks."

"That's right," Father said. "Aunt Anne and

I used to build sundials when we ran out of watches."

Terry bounced on his bare toes. "Tell us how!" he urged. His eyes searched the beach for sticks even before he knew how to use them.

"We need some string," Grandpa said.

"I'll get my string ball," Tom said. He trotted across the sand, pumping his arms.

"We need one strong forked stick, and twelve straight ones," Grandpa planned.

"May I borrow your knife, Father?" Terry asked. He slapped the pocket of his bathing trunks to show he did not swim with a knife in his pocket.

Swimming was forgotten while the Tuckers worked on a beach clock. Penny went with Grandpa to find his compass in the locker in the Tub. Merry brought the rake from the yard. She and Tina cleaned and smoothed a spot where the sun would shine on the ground from daybreak to sundown.

Tom brought a length of twine. Father showed him where to drive a stake. Then they dropped a loop of cord around the stake. A loop in the other end of the cord was placed around a marking stick. "Pull your string tight," Father told Tom. "Hold your marking stick straight up and go around in a circle."

Tom tried, but drew an oval.

"You're not drawing eggs," Father told Tom. "Make a circle for the face of the clock."

Tom tried several times. Each time he failed Penny and Merry helped him smooth the sand to try again. Finally Tom drew a perfect circle. Father said he couldn't have done better himself.

"We're ready for your forked stick, Terry!" Father shouted.

"One forked stick, coming up!" Terry shouted back.

"I'll boss the job," Father said. "Terry, pull up Tom's center stake. Put your forked stick in its place."

Busily Terry obeyed. "Now what?" he asked eagerly.

Next Father sent Terry to find a long stick as straight as a ruler. This took some time. While he was gone, Grandpa and Father whittled points on twelve small stakes.

When Terry brought a straight, strong stick, Father examined it. He squinted down its length as if he were sighting down a gun barrel. "Fine," Father decided. "This is our pointer. Now, our pointer has to point at the North Star."

Merry scanned the high blue sky. "Do we have to wait till night to make our clock?" she asked anxiously.

"Grandpa has a compass," Father said. "We'll let him put our pointer in place."

Terry hung over Grandpa's shoulder while he used the compass. It showed north, south, east, and west instead of the hour of the day. "Jim Jackson knows how to use a watch for a compass," Terry said. "He showed me how to find north."

"Handy thing to know," Grandpa agreed.

"But you have to have a watch that runs," Terry said, with a sly look at Merry.

At last Grandpa put the straight stick in the Y of the forked stick. "The pointer stick is pointing straight at the North Star," Grandpa said. "That is twelve o'clock, and on the opposite side of the circle is six o'clock."

"I know where three o'clock is," Tom said proudly. He was just learning to tell time. He pointed to a spot on the circle halfway between twelve and six.

Penny ran around the circle till she faced Tom. "This is nine o'clock," she said happily.

"Every day the sun shines," Grandpa told them, "the pointer will leave a shadow on the ground to tell the time."

Terry studied the circle Tom had drawn. "Now I know what the sticks are for," he said. "We have to divide the circle in twelve parts and poke the sticks in the ground to mark the hours."

Tom counted the sticks from one to twelve. He handed them to Terry while Father helped divide the circle.

When the last stick was pushed in, the Tuckers stood in an admiring circle to look at their clock in the sand. All afternoon they ran to the sun-dial to check the time.

"It works!" Terry crowed.

"Father and Grandpa said it would," Merry said pertly. "So of course it works!"

In a game of Keep-Away Terry forgot about

the sundial. He ran backward reaching for the beach ball. He almost stepped on the pointer stick.

"Did you bump it?" Tina asked anxiously. "It won't tell the truth if we bump it."

"No, I didn't touch it," Terry said with relief, "but it was a close call!"

"I'll fix that," Tom promised. Once more he ran to the cottage for his ball of twine. He spent the rest of the afternoon building a fence around their sundial. He drove sticks into the ground. He wound them with so much twine, only a few inches remained on his spool.

"Do you think Butch will see there's something inside my fence?" Tom asked.

"He couldn't miss it," Terry told Tom. He slapped his small brother on the shoulders. Leave it to Tom to fix things.

"I wonder where Butch is," Tina said. She had been clearing the beach of balls, towels, inner tubes, fins, suntan lotion, bathing caps, and clogs. Now she looked far down the beach. "We haven't seen him since morning."

Merry and Terry were setting up the huge

umbrella for Mother and Grandma. "I wouldn't blame him if he never came back," Merry muttered.

Terry flushed. All day he had felt a little guilty about making the rickermeracker tracks to scare Butch.

Now he had the mystery of the Arney house to worry about. Terry wished he could be sure he wouldn't get Butch in trouble by telling Grandpa about the trespassers.

9

Thieves!

Terry helped Merry place lounge chairs under the striped beach umbrella for Mother and Grandma. Tom carried a magazine and suntan lotion to Mother. Penny ran for Grandma's lap desk and note paper. Tina made a Thermos of iced tea.

"Thank you, children," Mother said. "You're pampering us. But we love it, don't we, Mother Tucker?"

"Indeed we do," Grandma said with a comfortable sigh. "What time is it? Somebody must remind me to knead the rolls for dinner."

Tina hugged Grandma. "You never forget, Grandma!" she insisted, loving the touch of

Grandma's cheek. Tina led the parade to the sundial to check the time. "Three hours till supper, Grandma," she called. She asked the rest of the Tuckers, "What shall we do?"

Merry stretched her hands high and yawned noisily. "Let's travel."

"Well, how about hunting for Grandpa's oar?" Terry suggested.

Penny looked worried. "What if we see the trespassers?" she asked.

"Or what if the trespassers see us?" Tom wanted to know.

"That's a good question, Tom," Terry agreed. "But we won't go near the Arney house. If the oar had been on their beach, we'd have seen it."

Terry was pilot. He started the motor and headed the bow of the Tub for the faraway red spot. It did not seem so far away when they knew where they were going.

Out of sight of the Arney house, they pulled the Tub up on the sand so it could not drift. Then they walked in the smooth cool sand where the waves slapped the beach at night. They walked a long way, but did not find the oar.

"Let's go back to the Tub and walk the other way," Merry suggested.

They walked in the opposite direction. Still they did not find the oar.

"Maybe it sank," Penny said.

If Merry or Tina had said that, Terry would have snorted. Since it was Penny he just said, "Oars don't sink. They float."

They walked as far as the old gray bath-house. "This is where we picked up Butch," Merry said.

Terry chewed his lip while he thought. If Tom and Penny could walk this beach without getting tired, so could Butch. And if Butch had an old brown horse, he could ride all the way to Grandpa's cottage in a very short time. It looked bad for Butch. He could be one of the prowlers at the Arney cottage.

Terry sighed unhappily. He did not want to suspect Butch. Butch was bashful and lonesome. But he did not seem like the kind of boy who would break into a house.

Then Terry thought of something else. Maybe Butch's father had broken into the Arney house.

Maybe a whole family lived in the red-and-white house this summer! There were a lot of food packages on the table.

Terry scrubbed his head to try to make the thought go away. But it would not go. Terry was glad when Tina called, "I've found something."

"Did you find the oar?" Tom shouted.

"No, I didn't find the oar," Tina called back. "But I've found something very odd!"

Tom, Penny, Merry, and Terry ran across the sand to the shady spot at the edge of the woods. There Tina was studying the ground. "Isn't that odd?" she asked. "Wheel marks in this old road."

"Where does the road go?" Tom asked.

"To an old farm," Terry told Tom. "Nobody has lived there as long as I can remember. I've been up to the old farm with Grandpa and Father lots of times. There's an old orchard. We always pick apples and Grandma makes pies."

All five Tuckers walked up the road. They bent their heads to study the tire marks. They reached a place where a path crossed the road. Tom found a deep print of a horse's hoof.

Merry walked ahead of the group. "Somebody has driven a lot of horses along this road," she called.

Terry loped to catch up with Merry. When he studied the ground he could see that some of the prints went up the road, while others went down the road. Only a few prints went past the path. The path followed the shoreline just above high-water mark.

"Not a lot of horses, Merry," Terry told his twin. "See that nicked place in the tip of a horse-shoe? One horse has walked on this road lots of times."

"Butch?" Merry asked. She widened her eyes and put both hands over her mouth. "That path goes to our house, doesn't it?"

Terry nodded. "Right to it," he agreed. He did not have to add, "From the Arney house." Merry could see that for herself.

"We'll have to tell Grandpa and Father, won't we?" Merry asked.

Unhappily, Terry agreed.

The twins stood close together while they waited for Tina to come up the old road. She was leading Tom and Penny. They were not walking

very fast. Tina looked worried.

"Betcha Tina figured out about Butch, too," Terry muttered.

"Let's not tell Father yet," Terry argued. "After all, we're just guessing. We don't *know* the Arney house has been broken into. They might have loaned it to friends who lost their keys. And," Terry finished with another brisk scrub on his head, "we don't even *know* Butch has a horse."

"Butch hasn't said anything about the horse, has he?" Merry asked slowly. Butch had just laughed when the Tuckers were scared by the noises in the night. And Butch had been afraid the rickermeracker might hurt the old brown horse. What did that prove? That Butch liked horses?

As Tina, Tom, and Penny drew even with the twins, Merry asked, "Are you getting too tired to walk some more, Penny?"

Penny's face was pink and damp looking. She looked tired.

"I think we'd better start home," Tina said. "We're dying to know who has been driving on the road, but we had better explore it some other day."

Terry and Merry did not argue. They were not sure they would like what they found at the end of the road.

When the Tuckers returned to the Tub they put on their life jackets and pushed off. Tina stood up in the middle to shove the boat into deeper water. Terry started the outboard motor.

"Wait till I check the gas," Terry warned. He shook the tank. There was a hollow, sloshing sound. The boat rocked as he walked to the bow to get the can of gas Father had placed there. But there was no can. Terry rummaged. Still he found no gas can. One article at a time, Terry removed the supplies stored under the bow. Then he sat back on his heels and said, "This beats all!"

"It has to be there," Merry insisted. "We all saw Father put the can in. We haven't used it. Cans don't walk away. Look again, Terry."

Again Terry searched, but there was no gas can.

Tina had been silent. Now she pointed at the beach. Bare footprints led to and from the deep cut in the sand where the heavy Tub had been beached.

"Somebody stole our gas!" Terry yelled.

"Do we have enough to get home?" Merry asked anxiously.

"If we go straight home, we can go in on fumes," Terry said crossly. He made fists of his hands while he examined the underbrush beyond the sand. "I'd just like to meet that guy."

"Maybe you're lucky you didn't meet him," Tina said mildly. "He might be twice your size. He has pretty big feet."

When they were halfway home Merry said unexpectedly, "Butch's feet are big. I noticed when he measured the rickermeracker's track this morning."

Terry glowered at Merry. He had noticed and remembered, too. He didn't want to suspect Butch, but evidence was piling up.

Far down the lake a boat flashed red in the late afternoon sun.

"That sounds like Arneys' motor," Terry said. He was tempted to investigate, but he did not dare waste the gas.

All five Tuckers strained to look and listen. "I think you're right, Terry," Tina said. "But they're so far away, I can't be sure."

From the many hours spent on the beach, the Tuckers had learned to recognize the shape and sound of the boats on Lake Annabelle.

"They're probably using our gas," Terry said sourly.

"They won't get far," Tom declared. "That's a big boat. It uses lots of gas."

"If they stole our gas can, what's to keep them from stealing more gas?" Merry asked.

Terry's eyes narrowed. "Or anything else they need," he added.

A cold silence that was hard to break settled over the Tuckers. It was hard for them to believe somebody would steal. When so many odd little things involved Butch, no one wanted to say the word that would accuse him.

Finally Tina said, "Shouldn't we tell the police our gas was stolen?"

Terry shrugged. "Why? The police don't work out here in the woods."

"Well, somebody does!" Merry declared.

"It's the sheriff," Tom said solidly.

"How do *you* know that?" Tina asked. With surprise she stared at the brother who was less than half her age.

"Easy," Tom said. "I just listen when men talk." Tom poked out his lower lip and bobbed his head. He looked like Father and Grandpa when they talked about their store, the newspaper or the Government. "You can learn a lot by listening," Tom said.

Tom turned his attention to the red boat, but Tina watched her small brother with respect. Each of the Tuckers was different. Tina herself liked to play the piano and write poetry. Terry was the clown of the family who liked to be in the middle of activities. Merry was half tomboy, half lady. Penny looked fragile enough to break. But Tom had a brain that clicked twenty-four hours a day.

"See?" Tom said. "I told you they would run out of gas. That boat has stopped."

"Look!" Tina gasped. "Somebody is diving out of that boat!"

"Must be a good swimmer, to leave the boat

that far from shore," Merry declared.

"And stupid!" Terry snorted. "Nobody but an idiot would leave a boat adrift."

"Unless it doesn't belong to them," Tina said thoughtfully. "If they stole it, what difference would it make if they ruined it?"

10
"Find My Feet!"

Tina and Merry were reading under the striped umbrella when Grandpa roared. Tina dropped her book. Merry sat up straight and peeped under the edge of the umbrella.

"My goodness," Merry said in an awed whisper. "When Grandpa is unhappy, everybody knows it!"

Tina looked worried. "Oh-oh, I hope he isn't mad at us."

"Oh, Tina!" Merry retorted. "As if he ever is."

"What does that Todd Arney use for *brains?*" Grandpa bellowed.

"See? I told you he wasn't mad at us," Merry declared, but she sighed with relief.

Both girls left their books and ran down the beach.

They found Grandpa just beyond the willows where they usually spread their towels during rest hour. The Arneys' red boat rocked in shallow water. Grandpa was sitting on a stone, taking off his shoes.

"Oh, the poor boat!" Tina cried.

"It's slapping its bottom out on the rocks," Merry said. She waded into the water and heaved at the bow. The heavy boat was wedged in sand and stones.

Terry and Tom crashed through the brushy undergrowth which separated the cottage yard from the beach.

"We heard you, Grandpa!" Terry yelled. "Do you need help?"

"I certainly do need help," Grandpa declared grimly. "And that Todd Arney is going to need some help, too, if ever I get my hands on him. Imagine treating his father's boat like that!" Grandpa scowled at the long, sleek boat which was now rubbed raw below its waterline.

Solemnly Tom declared, "That'll need more

than a paint job." He waded into the water and bent down to poke his fingers into splintery wood. "This boat needs a new bottom."

Terry ran to find Father. In a few minutes the whole family gathered on the beach to rescue Arneys' boat. Grandma and Penny sat on the beach. Everybody else waded into the water. With much lifting and shifting, they raised the boat from the rocks and set it afloat.

"It leaks," Tom declared.

"But not much," Terry said. He joined his smaller brother to examine every scar on the boat. "We can tow it back to the Arney dock." He turned to Father. "Do we have time before lunch?"

"Don't be gone too long," Father said.

"I don't understand this," Grandpa stated flatly. "There was no storm last night. Why should this boat have gone adrift?" With one wrinkled hand he smoothed its bow, as if he petted an injured dog.

Before returning to their job of painting the window trim, Grandpa and Father helped the children tie the Arney boat in towing position.

Tina was pilot. Terry, too, sat in the stern. He checked the tow rope. Merry sat between Tom and Penny in the center seat.

"Why didn't we tell Grandpa about the gas can?" Tom asked.

"Because we weren't *sure*," Tina explained. "We just *thought* the people who stole our gas might have taken the boat."

"Well, now I'm sure," Terry said stubbornly.

Tina looked thoughtful. "I don't see how Butch could have anything to do with stealing the gas," she said. "He's afraid of boats. Remember, Terry, how he sat in the bottom of the Tub and hung onto the floor boards? He would never have nerve enough to jump into the middle of the lake."

"Especially when there is a paddle in the boat," Merry added.

The Tuckers agreed. A frightened boy would not dive. He would paddle, no matter how long it took to reach shore.

They wanted to trust Butch. But how could they, when there had been no trouble before Terry found him on the beach? Slowly they crossed the bay. As they came near the Arney dock, Terry stood up and shaded his eyes against the sun.

"Looks pretty deserted," he said.

Terry knew how to tie knots to hold the red boat in place. They dropped the long hard-rubber bumpers overboard to keep the boat from rubbing the edge of the dock.

When they were sure there was nothing else they could do to protect the red boat, they went home. Merry started a song to break the gloom which had settled over them when they saw the Arney house.

At their own dock, Tom was the first out of his life jacket. "I'll go look at the sun clock," he offered. "Maybe we have time to play ball before lunch."

"Good idea," Tina agreed. "I feel like stretching my legs."

Down the length of the dock and along the catwalk, Tom ran.

Carefully Tom studied the shadow line the pointer stick left on the ground. Then he counted pegs to find the hour.

"Halfway between eleven and twelve," he shouted.

Suddenly a large shadow darkened the ground. Tom looked up, expecting to see Father. Instead, he saw two tall boys. One was blond, the other dark. The blond boy circled the sun clock. The one with black eyes whistled and looked over Tom's head. He pretended not to see Tom, the dial, or the fence Tom had built. He walked right through the sundial and kicked stakes as if he walked through tall grass.

Tom stamped his feet with anger. He ran after the tall boy and grabbed his belt. Furiously, he hung on. "You come back here!" he roared. "You can't break our clock."

The tall boy laughed. "Looks like I did!" he taunted.

"Terry!" Tom shrieked. "Father! Grandpa! Help!"

"You wait till my father catches you, Muscle Man!" Terry yelled, running ahead of Tina and Merry. He, too, shouted, "Help! Help!"

"Tattletale," Muscle Man jeered. His black eyes shone. His mouth poked out in a sneer. But the thin blond boy looked embarrassed.

"Hey!" Father yelled from the cottage yard. "What's going on?"

The tall boy hesitated, as if he were deciding whether or not to stay and fight. He turned and ran down the beach. Both teen-agers followed the path at high-water line which led to the Arney house.

Grandpa, Father, Mother, and Grandma joined the children at the scene of the ruined sun-dial.

"We'll build another one," Grandpa said to comfort the unhappy Tuckers.

"You'll have to find north, Grandpa," Tom reminded him. Busily he began untangling his string. He wound it on a piece of stick.

During the hour after lunch Merry, Terry, and Tom helped Grandpa rebuild the sand clock. Tom built a taller and stronger fence.

While they rested from their afternoon swim, the adults played bridge on the beach table. Tom couldn't find his stilts or mitt so he roamed the beach to pick up dead fish that had drifted ashore. These he buried. Sugar chased grass-hoppers in the clumps of sedge which grew in the sand near the water.

Under the big umbrella Merry and Tina read. Penny made a necklace of the joint grass. Terry raced with Toby. When he tired, he dropped to the sand near the umbrella.

Terry scooped sand till he had a hole large enough to bury his legs. Then he covered them and patted the sand into a smooth mound. "Find my feet," he ordered Toby. Toby dog-laughed, shook his woolly head till his ears flopped, and raced in circles around Terry.

"Find my feet!" Terry commanded.

"I'll grant that Toby is smart, but he has to have some inkling of what you want him to do," Father called. "Show him your feet."

Hastily Terry uncovered his bare legs. Then he wiggled his toes and stuck them close to Toby's nose. "Feet," he said. "Find my feet!" He put only a little sand on his feet and wiggled his toes.

With a joyous bark Toby jumped and planted his big front paws over Terry's feet.

Once in a while Merry and Tina glanced up from their books to watch Terry train Toby in the new trick. Soon Toby was digging till the

sand flew whenever Terry ordered him, "Find my feet."

"Let's see if he will find my feet," Merry said, joining her twin.

Toby did not hesitate. He started digging before Merry had finished covering her legs.

Tina tilted the umbrella until the edge touched the ground. Then she pushed one foot under the edge and wiggled her toes. "Find my feet," she told Toby. Instantly Toby bounced forward and scooped such a big hole he crawled under the umbrella.

"That's pretty smart!" Terry declared. He tousled Toby's shaggy head.

"That trick might come in handy some time," Father said, joining the children. He petted Toby, then added, "Grandma wants to know where you'd like to eat supper."

"On the beach, of course!" Terry declared. On the long sunny days of summer no Tucker stayed inside four walls when he could be out-of-doors.

Father did not have to tell the Tuckers to help Grandma and Mother set the table and carry food to the beach. They picnicked so often each knew just what to do to be helpful.

"Mmm, smell those baked beans!" Terry said. He sniffed hungrily when he set down the brown bean pot.

"Tina made the potato salad," Penny said. "Isn't it pretty?"

Tom carried the napkin-covered breadbasket. "Cinnamon buns, just out of the oven," he announced. "I'm so hungry, I wanted to hide and eat all of them."

"When I was your age, I did just that," Terry admitted with an embarrassed laugh.

"Did you, Terry?" Both Tom and Penny looked surprised to learn that Terry had not always been a big brother.

Suddenly Terry cocked his head. His face became blank with listening.

"I heard that sound, too," Merry said with a giggle. "It wasn't a rickermeracker. It was a horse."

"That's what I thought," Terry said. "But why would a horse be down by the sundial?"

Instantly the five Tuckers raced around the slight curve of the beach to the sundial. They were just in time to see the old brown horse crash through the underbrush. A boy was on the horse. A blond boy.

Tom looked ready to cry. "He ruined it!" he wailed. "Twice in one day. That's too much!"

Terry clenched his fists and stared at the tumbled sticks. "This isn't funny," he declared loudly. "I only made rickermeracker tracks. I didn't break up anything that belonged to Butch."

"D-Do you think—?" Tina stammered.

"Sure, I think!" Terry interrupted. "I think Butch is getting even with me for scaring him."

"I—don't—know," Tina said slowly. "The boy on the horse was blond, but we didn't see his face."

"I'll bet you that horse doesn't belong to the boy," Merry said unexpectedly.

Both Tina and Terry stared at her. "How do you know?" Terry asked.

"That horse didn't act happy," Merry said, bobbing her head.

Terry snorted, "Happy horses!"

"I see what Merry means," Tina told Terry.

"That horse was swinging his head as if he didn't like his rider. He was acting like Toby does sometimes when a stranger tries to touch him."

"Well, I don't like him either," Terry said stubbornly. "We have to build the sundial again."

Grandma came down the beach path with a pot of coffee. She paused long enough to sympathize with the angry Tuckers. She had a sure cure for every trouble. "Come to supper," she invited. "You'll feel better after you have eaten."

Tina took the coffeepot from Grandma's hands. Grandma walked between Tom and Penny. Merry and Terry drew a line in the sand. They raced to the table.

Suddenly a roar as loud as Grandpa's split the air. "Our food!" Terry bellowed. "It's gone!"

11
Mr. Wilson's Trouble

"Gone?" Grandma repeated. "Terry, look around. Maybe somebody is playing a trick on you."

"Fat trick!" Terry yelled angrily. "Stealing our supper!"

Merry ran back to meet Grandma, who walked as fast as she could over the sand. "Our food is really gone, Grandma," Merry insisted stormily.

Father came down the path, combing his hair. He stuck his comb in his shirt pocket and asked, "What's the uproar?"

"Tighten your belt, Father," Terry advised sourly. "There's no supper."

"What do you mean, no supper?" Grandpa

asked, as he followed Mother down the beach path. "I took the baked beans out of the oven with my own hands."

Unable to believe their eyes, the whole Tucker family stood around the table where empty plates sat.

Penny's lips quivered. "I'm hungry," she said in a small voice.

"If Penny is hungry, the rest of you must be starved," Grandma said sympathetically. Briskly she began to stack plates. "We'll just go back to the cottage and eat pancakes!"

"Pick up your plate and walk!" Father said, winking at Tom.

In the cottage kitchen Grandma mixed the batter. Tina heated the griddle and turned the cakes. Mother fried bacon and drained it on a paper towel. Merry filled the fruit bowls with spicy applesauce. Penny bit the tip of her tongue while she set the bowls on the table. Terry poured milk. Tom carried butter and maple syrup from the cupboard.

While they worked, they talked about the mystery of the missing picnic food. Who had taken the food? Why? Where had they been hiding? How had they known about the beach table?

"I think that horse has something to do with it," Terry said, scowling.

"How could it?" Merry argued. "The horse was on the opposite end of the beach."

"Terry may be right," Father said. "It would take two people to carry the food. One could have drawn attention away from the table by breaking up the sundial."

"Yeah," Terry agreed. "And Butch is the only one we've ever seen with the old brown horse."

The Tuckers looked at each other with questioning eyes. Was Butch a thief? They didn't want that to be true.

"I wish I hadn't made those darned rickermeracker tracks," Terry muttered to Tina. "I didn't know Butch would try to get even."

"Maybe he didn't," Tina said thoughtfully. She set a platter of pancakes on the table and turned to the windows. From the top of a slight slope she could see the torn-up sundial. In the distance the red spot near shore was the Arney house. There were open spots along the shore where she could see the line of the path. Since Butch had appeared out of nowhere, the shore had become the stage for a mystery.

Tina liked puzzles. When a new shipment of jigsaw puzzles arrived at the store, Grandpa always brought home the hardest one for her to put together on a card table. The small pieces of this mystery were like the odd-shaped parts of a jigsaw puzzle.

But how did they fit together? A boy, always alone, who did not tell where he lived. An old brown horse. Burning cartons on a hidden beach. Pebbles flipped from a tree. Tracks on an unused road. Stolen food. Stolen gas. A drifting boat. A house being used by somebody who was never seen. A broken sundial.

Nothing more was said about the stolen food, but suspicion remained. It made Tina feel uneasy. Butch had not been back since the rickermeracker trick.

While they washed dishes Merry whispered to Tina, "We have to write the you-know-whats tonight."

"What's a you-know-what?" Tina asked, still

puzzling over the pieces of her mystery.

"The invitations to our floating fire party, of course," Merry replied.

Tina put the last dish in the cupboard, then reminded Merry, "We haven't asked Grandma and Mother if we may have a party."

"We *always* have company on the Fourth," Merry argued.

Mother returned to the kitchen in time to hear Merry's statement.

"And why not?" she asked cheerfully. "The more, the merrier."

"Do you mean that, Mother?" Merry asked. Her eyes sparkled and she crossed her fingers behind her back. "May we have a big bonfire and a wiener roast?"

"That sounds like fun," Mother agreed. "But you must check with Grandma. She may have other plans."

"I'll ask her now," Merry cried. She darted into the living room where the family was gathered around the portable television set. Almost at once she returned to the kitchen. "Grandma says Yes," she told Tina. She made up a dance. She tapped her way across the room to rummage for note paper in the big cupboard.

Merry and Tina spent the evening in the trailer with the door locked. Finally Tina composed an invitation which pleased Merry. With great care they copied it, over and over. They addressed envelopes to Aunt Anne, to all the lake neighbors who had provided milk cartons, to all the employees of Tuckers' Variety Store, and to their town neighbors, the Jacksons and the Corbetts.

Unable to control their curiosity, Tom, Penny, and Terry made countless trips to tap on the

trailer door. Each time Merry cried, "Go 'way, we're busy." When the last invitation was folded and sealed in its envelope, Merry threw open the door. Terry sat so close to the door, he almost fell into the trailer. "You didn't have to leave me out," he complained.

Merry shrugged. "You always spill ink," she retorted.

To make peace Tina told Terry he could mail the invitations.

The next morning the three older Tuckers were first to excuse themselves from the breakfast table. Terry carried the invitations while they hurried up the short-cut path through the woods.

"No new tire tracks by the mailbox," Terry declared. "The mailman hasn't been here."

While they waited Terry drew a hopscotch court. They threw flat pebbles into the squares. Terry stepped on the lines when he hopped. Merry giggled so hard her pebble rolled. Tina won the game just as the mail truck came in sight.

Right behind the mail truck was Mr. Wilson's

milk truck. "Let's ride with Mr. Wilson," Terry suggested. "Maybe he has found the Smiths!"

"O.K., flag him while I mail the letters," Merry agreed.

There was no noisy, cheerful greeting when Terry, Merry, and Tina climbed into the truck. Merry asked anxiously, "Is something wrong, Mr. Wilson?"

The man sighed. "It's one of those days when things go wrong," he said, frowning at the road. "Several customers have complained about no milk delivery. I don't understand it. I never skip customers."

"You've never skipped us, Mr. Wilson," Merry declared. "That would cause a mess at our house. We drink gallons of milk!"

Mr. Wilson looked happier. "You Tuckers are good customers," he agreed. "But so are a lot of other summer residents. There is no grocery store to run to five minutes before breakfast. So I try to give good service."

"That's the way we manage our business," Terry said. "We Tuckers give good service at our variety store."

When they came in sight of Green Fields, both Merry and Tina watched for Mrs. Fields and her baby. They were disappointed when they saw that nobody waited at the back gate.

Terry jumped out of the truck and fished in the box on the gatepost for the order slip. "Two quarts of milk, a pint of whipping cream, and a carton of cottage cheese," he read. Terry gathered up the food and carefully set Mrs. Fields's order in the box on the gatepost.

"Won't the milk spoil when the sun hits it?" Tina asked anxiously when they were again rolling down the shaded road.

"Mrs. Fields will pick it up when she takes her baby for a walk in the sun," Mr. Wilson replied.

The Tuckers rode to the end of the route, and back again. When they came in sight of Green Fields, they saw Mrs. Fields waiting beside the road. The baby sat in a stroller that had green fringe around its sunshade.

"Ooh," Tina breathed. "We'll get to see the baby after all!"

"That baby is a corker," Mr. Wilson agreed.

With a broad smile he stopped the milk truck. His smile died when Mrs. Fields burst out, "So you've skipped us again! Yesterday I thought it was an accident, so I used canned milk for the baby's formula. But today I have no canned milk, and my baby is hungry!"

Wide-eyed, the Tuckers listened to the angry young woman.

The Tuckers owned a store. They knew the business rule, "The customer is always right." Still Terry burst out in Mr. Wilson's defense. "I read your order, Mrs. Fields. And I put your milk and cheese and cream in the box."

"I saw him," Merry said, bobbing her dark head earnestly.

Mrs. Fields was too much upset to listen. "This isn't the first time milk has been missing," she insisted. "Some of my neighbors have been skipped, too. All I can say is, if you're not to be depended on, Mr. Wilson, you can just take me off your list. I'll buy my milk from somebody else!"

With a worried frown Mr. Wilson listened to Mrs. Fields's angry complaint. The baby made little fretful sounds. She stopped to pat him on the back. Mr. Wilson asked, "Mrs. Fields, will you please give me the names of my customers who have failed to get their milk?"

"I certainly will!" Mrs. Fields retorted. Her eyes flashed as she gave the names of her neighbors.

"Thank you," Mr. Wilson said gravely. He lifted two quarts of milk from a case and asked Terry to find the whipping cream and cheese. "There will be no charge today, Mrs. Fields. If you will figure out how many quarts you have failed to get, I'll take the amount off your bill. Fair enough?"

Mrs. Fields's anger cooled down. "Of course that's fair, Mr. Wilson." A little doubtfully she glanced at Terry. "You *did* say you delivered milk, cream, and cheese, Terry. You wouldn't have known what I ordered if you hadn't read my list." She threw out her hands and demanded, "If you delivered it, what happened to my order?"

Mr. Wilson took off his striped cap. He wiped the white strip of his forehead which was never

exposed to the sun. "I am sure I don't know, Mrs. Fields, but I am going to find out before I lose all my customers."

The Tuckers went with Mr. Wilson when he called on the angry customers. All of the people Mrs. Fields had named were just as upset as she.

They rode back to the short-cut path with the worried milkman. Silently Tina shifted the parts of her puzzle. There was a new piece to be added. Stolen dairy products.

Stolen gas. Stolen food. Stolen milk. A house being used. Somebody must be stealing a living instead of working for it. But—who?

Not the people who owned the cottages. They had been living on Lake Annabelle for as many summers as Tina could recall.

But what about the mysterious Smiths who had no mailbox? Where did they live? Butch had never mentioned his father. How did Mr. Smith earn a living for his family?

Tina's cheeks burned as she tried to shake her suspicions out of her mind. No matter how hard she tried, a little voice inside her head whispered, "Smith. Butch Smith."

When Tina, Merry, and Terry returned to Grandpa's cottage, the house was vacant. They could hear sounds on the beach. Down the path they ran. The action they saw was familiar. Every summer Father and Grandpa moved the boat dock into deeper water as the water went down from use and evaporation. Today both Grandpa and Father stood on the dock. They wore their swim trunks and used long poles. They pushed the heavy platform like a raft.

The rest of the family watched from shore. Tom walked up and down like a foreman.

"Oh!" Terry said with disappointment. "I

wanted to help move the dock." He cupped his hands and yelled, "Need some help?"

"Sure!" Father answered cheerfully. "Come give a hand."

Terry ran into the woods and returned with a pole. It was white and smooth from rain and sun. With a whoop he waded into Lake Annabelle. When the water reached Terry's chin, he swam with legs and one arm and floated the pole. Dad put down a hand to boost Terry onto the dock.

From the shore Merry and Tina watched. Tina thought the three looked like pioneer rivermen, rafting down the Mississippi. Father chanted "Yo, heave, ho!" each time they pushed. Suddenly his pole snapped. He staggered to keep from falling backward.

"You can use my pole," Terry offered.

Father picked up one of the oars which lay flat on the dock. "Keep your pole, Terry," he said. "I'll just brace this oar against a piling and push."

A piling was a heavy stake driven into the bottom of the lake, to hold the boat dock in place.

From the shore Tom called soberly, "Better be careful, Father. Grandpa says don't push with the oars. They break."

"I'll be careful, Tom," Father promised. He turned to Terry and Tom. "Ready for the countdown?"

"Ready!" Terry whooped.

"One, two, three, *push!*" Father counted and pushed. With a cracking noise the oar he used broke. The paddle end fell in the water. "Well," Father said, dropping the useless round handle on the dock.

For a long second nobody made a sound. Then as if they answered a signal, the five children burst out laughing.

"You looked so funny, Father!" Merry squealed.

"Anyway, the dock is out far enough," Terry said.

"We're hard on oars," Tom declared. "Now we *have* to find the oar we lost!"

12
Playing Detective

The Tuckers waited until Father and Grandpa snapped the chains onto the pilings to anchor the dock. Father laid the ramp across the water to the sand like a slanting bridge. Then to Mother he called, "How about a cup of coffee, honey?"

Tom hitched up the belt of his red shorts. "We'd better go hunt for that oar," he declared.

"It's almost lunchtime," Mother reminded as she started toward the cottage to make coffee for the men.

"May we carry sandwiches?" Tina asked.

"I have a ham I can slice," Grandma planned. "Ham makes a good sandwich."

"Peanut butter for me," Tom said.

Grandma repeated, "Peanut butter for Tom," like a waitress taking an order. The whole family smiled. Tom ate peanut butter even on pancakes.

Tina and Merry helped Grandma make up five small packages of lunch. When they gathered on the boat dock, Merry looked at the padded life jackets with distaste. "It's too hot to wear those things," she declared.

"Then let's not," Tina said.

"Oh, Tina!" Merry widened her eyes. "Grandpa would skin us alive if we went out in the Tub without our life preservers."

"We won't have to wear them if we walk the shore," Tina said calmly. "We can't find the oar with the boat. Let's search the shore."

"Sounds like a good idea," Terry agreed at once. "All in favor?"

"Aye!" the Tuckers chorused and ran down the ramp.

"Here, Toby, here, Toby!" Tina shouted.

Toby left his favorite resting place under the willows where the children liked to spread their towels. Toby was a large dog with black and white fur. In hot weather he hunted shade, and there he rested his big head on his front paws and watched his family with bright, beady eyes. The minute Tina called, Toby loped across the sand. His curls waved like flags. His feet thumped the ground.

"Sounds like a horse," Terry declared with a grin. Toby's size was a Tucker joke. Dad insisted they had moved from a city apartment to the big house in Yorkville to give Toby space to grow.

"Good old Toby," Tina said when Toby fell in step with the Tuckers. "Now, stay with us. No chasing chipmunks or rabbits."

"Are we scared?" Penny asked. Worriedly she looked out over the beach and water.

"Well—maybe," Tina admitted.

Tina's words quieted the Tuckers. For some time they followed the path along the shore line without making much noise. They talked about the mysterious milk thief and the stolen picnic food. But by the time they were close enough to see the shape of the Arney house, they were whooping with their usual noisy cheerfulness.

The twins walked the beach most of the time,

searching for the oar. Every few minutes they scrambled back onto the path to join Tina, Tom, and Penny.

They reached the old road which led to the deserted farm. By this time wind and an occasional night-patter of rain had almost erased the tire marks. But there were new marks of a horse's hoofs. They had noticed the same mark with a nick in the horseshoe all along the path. And when they came in sight of the bathhouse, they saw the old brown horse tied to a tree. He stood on three feet and hung his head down as if he had been there for some time.

Terry's lips tightened. "I'm going to see if Butch is around here someplace," he declared. "After breaking up our sundial with that horse, he has some explaining to do!"

"I'll go with you," Merry said at once.

"Then I'll stay here with Penny and Tom," Tina decided. "Penny has walked far enough without a rest. And I know Tom is hungry. Aren't you, Tom?"

"Yes!" Tom admitted. Each Tucker carried his own lunch tied to his belt. Tom sat down and opened his brown paper bag. With sober enjoyment he began to eat his peanut butter sandwich.

"If we don't come back by the time Penny is rested," Merry told Tina, "send Toby to track us."

Merry meant the words as a joke, but Tina's eyes darkened with concern. "Something *could* happen," Tina reminded her.

"Don't worry, we'll be careful," Terry promised. He darted away. His rubber-soled sneakers made no noise on the path.

Merry and Terry did not have to talk. They were so used to each other, and so alike in their actions, each seemed to know what the other was going to do. Without making a plan, they ran down the path to the Arney house.

First they went to the dock to look at the boat they had rescued. The boat had been used again. Fishing tackle lay in a tangled mess. Somebody had cleaned fish on the end of the dock.

A little cautiously they circled the house. They looked through windows. Beds were tumbled. Dirty dishes and open cans sat on the table.

"Ssh!" Merry warned. She flattened her ear against a window.

"What is it?" Terry whispered. He pushed his face close to Merry's and listened, too.

In some room of the Arney house a radio was on. The announcer was forecasting rain for the Fourth of July. Worriedly the twins looked at each other. Which was worse: To find that Butch was living in the Arney house, or, to learn that their floating fire party might be rained out?

Merry shaded her eyes with one hand and peered at the sky. "There isn't a cloud," she said at last.

"That announcer is all mixed up," Terry said positively. "You know Grandpa says he listens to the weather forecast, then plans for the opposite kind of weather. The sun will shine all day on the Fourth."

"Well, good," Merry said, as if she agreed that the weather would be good because Terry said so. "Ssh!" she warned. Suddenly she realized that she had spoken aloud.

"Ssh, yourself," Terry retorted. "You're making all the noise." He nudged Merry's elbow.

"We'd better get out of here. I think I hear somebody coming."

Cautiously Terry and Merry edged around the porch. They hid in the boat storage room. Over their heads floor boards quivered. Little specks of dust loosened. They floated in a streak of light coming through a crack. Merry almost held her breath while she examined the dim space. Was there something in this room the owner of the feet might need? With relief she decided they were safe. Then she felt a tickle in her nose.

"I'm going to sneeze," she whispered.

"Sh," Terry whispered back, almost soundlessly. "There's somebody on the porch."

"It's a man, I think," Merry said, after listening to the weight of the steps. She pinched her nose. She tightened her lips till her cheeks puffed out.

"Don't do it," Terry warned.

Merry drew a deep breath.

"Are you all right now?" Terry asked.

"I swallowed my sneeze," Merry told him.

A porch step squeaked. There was a pause, then the weight was lifted from the step. The feet moved across the porch and into the house. Terry wiped his forehead.

"How long will we have to stay here?" Merry asked anxiously.

"If we don't go back, Tina will send Toby after us," Terry reminded her.

Merry's sigh was shaky. "I wouldn't mind seeing good old Toby," she said, a little wistfully.

When Terry decided it was safe, the twins left their hiding place under the Arneys' front porch. Their sneakers made no sound on the beaten path. Warily they watched windows until they were well out of sight of the house. As they came near the bathhouse, a nickering sound told them the old brown horse was still tied to a tree.

"I know Butch is around here someplace," Terry said with a frown, "or that horse wouldn't be here."

"Maybe Butch is in the bathhouse," Merry suggested. "If he had been fishing, he might want to clean up."

They tiptoed around the unpainted small building. They saw nothing unusual.

"I think I'll try the door," Terry said.

"O.K," Merry agreed. "There isn't a window to peek through."

"Who needs a window in a bathhouse!" Terry retorted. He put his hand on the doorknob. Merry stood close beside him.

"Go on," she urged. "Butch won't bite you."

Terry swallowed a lump in his throat. "I just happened to think," he admitted, "I might find something in here besides Butch. We don't know why that man was walking on the porch."

"Oh-oh, that's right," Merry agreed. "Let's—"

Merry had no chance to finish her sentence. Unexpectedly something hot and scratchy covered her head. Hands held her arms against her sides. She heard a "glub-blub" gasp from Terry. She felt a sharp blow on one of her ankles. Merry kicked with all her strength. The person who held her was tall enough to avoid her feet.

A hinge creaked. Merry felt herself pushed forward. She landed in a tumble. The minute her hands were free, she began to punch and was punched right back.

Merry rolled away and unwrapped her head. With amazement she stared back at Terry, who

had also uncovered his head. Both held sweaters in their hands.

"You hit me!" Merry accused.

"Well, you hit me first," Terry said hotly.

"Let's not fight," Merry urged. "We have to get out of here."

When her eyes got used to the dark, Merry examined the room in which she found herself. Obviously, Butch was not here. There was no window, and the door had no glass pane. Last year's bathing suits dangled from hooks around the bare wooden walls. Somebody had left a big beach towel on a bar. Soap on a cord hung from the shower head. A red and white beach ball had lost its air. It was a bright heap of plastic in one corner. A pair of water skis leaned against the wall of the shower in the opposite corner.

"Looks like we're stuck," Terry said soberly.

Both Merry and Terry got to their feet. Merry rubbed one knee while she tried to discover some way to get out of the room. Suddenly she giggled. She wrinkled her nose when she said, "We haven't tried the door. Probably we can open it and walk right out!"

"Betcha we can't," Terry said sourly.

Merry turned the knob. Then she pushed and kicked. The door would not budge. "You might help me," she told Terry.

"What good would that do?" Terry asked, shrugging. "The door is locked."

"Well, how are we going to get out?" Merry asked loudly.

Again Terry shrugged. But he began to circle the room to study the walls and floor. He stopped in one corner and stamped. "These boards feel spongy," he told Merry. "They might break."

Merry, too, bounced on the rotting floor boards. For a minute she felt a thrill of hope. Then she said darkly, "There's nothing under a floor but dirt. What do we do after we break the boards? We haven't anything to dig with, and it's a long way to China." She ended with a shaky laugh, but Terry did not laugh in return.

Since they had nothing else to do, they jumped up and down on the spongy wood.

"We could break a leg," Terry said.

"I s'pose we could," Merry agreed unhappily. "But that's not much worse than starving."

"Who's going to starve?" Terry asked. "I have my lunch tied to my belt."

"So have I!" Merry said with relief. "Let's eat!"

While they ate they tried to figure out why they had been pushed into the bathhouse. But finally they gave up.

"This is what we get for snooping," Merry said. She felt a rise of spirit now that she had eaten. "We can spend the night here if we have to. That towel is almost as big as a blanket, and we can put on these sweaters. If we get thirsty, we'll get a drink of water from the sink."

"Yeah," Terry agreed. "Father and Grandpa will hunt all night after Tina tells them where we left her. They'll find us. You wait and see."

"I—I know," Merry said wistfully. "But I wish they were already hunting for us."

The twins jumped some more on the only weak spot in the floor. Then Merry gave up. She folded the sweater which had covered her head. She sat on it and leaned against the wall with her arms folded. She scowled fiercely. No matter how hard she looked, there was no change in the room.

There was no window to break and no tool to use.

Terry, however, picked up one of the water skis. He whistled off-key. His face went blank, the way it did when he was really thinking. Merry watched him hopefully. When Terry was around, if a thing was movable, it moved!

He bounced the ski on its pointed tip. It made a dent in the floor.

"Fiberglas," he said approvingly. "A good ski."

"Well?" Merry said.

"I hope it doesn't break," Terry said. He raised his eyebrows at Merry to let her know only an idiot could possibly fail to see why he worried about Todd Arney's ski.

Wisely Merry said nothing.

Terry carried one of the skis to the spongy spot in the floor and pounded. Deep cuts appeared in the wet-looking gray wood. Merry jumped up and examined the floor. Then she, too, pounded with a ski.

Their foreheads dampened with perspiration. They were panting when Terry decided the floor was better than he had hoped.

"Let's not give up," Merry urged. "There are cracks between the boards. Maybe we can pry a piece loose if we both work on the same board."

"Maybe," Terry agreed.

Side by side on the same board, they used the skis like levers. After many attempts they managed to break a hole big enough to insert the tips of the skis. Then each put his whole weight on a ski.

Suddenly both Terry and Merry fell with the skis in their laps. A chunk of wood flipped into the air. It hit a wall and dropped.

"We did it!" Terry yelled.

A stale odor rose from a small hole in the floor.

"Ugh, I'll bet there are crickets under the floor," Merry said. She made a face and shivered.

"Who cares?" Terry asked. "The next piece will be easier to break out. We have room to work now."

Merry had never worked harder in her life. Bit by bit the hole grew larger. With every piece they broke loose, her spirit rose. Merry began to hum the cockroach song she had practiced so long on her violin.

Terry chuckled. "I always wondered about the words of that song. Now I know what they mean." Noisily he began to sing, "La Cuca*ra*cha, la Cuca*ra*cha, *How* I ache in ev'ry *bone*. I'm tired of *walk*ing, I'm tired of *talk*ing, *And* I wish to be a*lone*."

Merry sang, too, but she giggled and said, "I can make up a better verse." Very loudly she sang, "Oh, little Crick*et*, oh little Crick*et*, *How* I ache in ev'ry *bone*. I'm tired of *jab*bing, I'm tired of *stab*bing, I don't want to be a*lone*!"

Suddenly Terry straightened. He balanced Todd Arney's water ski on its tip. "Listen!" he ordered.

Someplace nearby a dog barked.

"Toby!" Merry gasped. "Tina has sent him to track us."

"Fat lot of good that does us," Terry said. "He's outside, and we're inside." He studied the hole they had broken in the floor. "You know what? I'll betcha we can crawl through that hole now."

"And land on our heads," Merry reminded.

"We can dig," Terry retorted. "We can poke

the dirt loose with the skis. Then we can scoop it out with our hands. That floor sill is only a two-by-four, and there's no cement under it."

"It will take all afternoon," Merry said.

"So what?" Terry wanted to know. "Now we know we can get out if we work hard enough."

"And we'll have Toby for company," Merry added.

"Yeah," Terry agreed. "He can scare off those big guys who dumped us in here."

"That's right," Merry said. Her throat tightened when she remembered the sweater over her head.

Terry whistled and Merry called, "Toby, To*by! Here*, boy!"

Almost at once they could hear Toby whine. The sound traveled around the bathhouse. They knew Toby must be nosing their footprints.

Merry tapped on the wall by the hole in the floor. "In here, Toby," Merry called.

Toby answered with a bark. There was a scratching sound on the wall.

"If Toby is so smart, why doesn't he dig under the wall instead of scratching?" Terry grumbled.

He picked up a ski and punched some holes in the black dirt. Then he scooped a little pile of dirt onto the floor. Merry knelt beside him to scoop dirt with her hands. While she worked she talked to Toby. It made her feel better, just to know Toby was outside the wall.

Each time they spoke, Toby scratched and whined.

"That's an awful lot of scratching going to waste," Terry complained. He clapped dirt from his hands and rested for a minute.

Suddenly Merry remembered the way Toby had dug under the rim of the umbrella.

"Maybe Toby can help us dig," she said excitedly.

Terry shrugged. "He could if he knew where to dig," he agreed.

"He'll know," Merry said positively. "I'll tell him!"

Terry bobbed his dark head and pushed out his lips. "Oh, sure," he said. "You'll just say, 'Please, Toby, count the boards. Dig under the seventh board from the corner closest to the old brown horse!' "

"Don't be silly," Merry retorted. "I can tell him where to dig." She crossed her fingers and added, "I hope!"

Merry tapped the wall by the hole. "Toby," she ordered, "find my feet!"

13
Angry Tuckers

"Find my feet!" Merry ordered, then begged, as Toby scratched on the outer wall of the old bathhouse.

"Nuts!" Terry said with disgust. "Toby doesn't know what you want him to do, so why waste your time? Come on, help me dig some more."

"I'll help in a minute," Merry said. "Toby can do it. He just has to figure out where we are."

Patiently she tapped the walls and coaxed, "Find my feet, Toby. Dig, boy!"

Terry punched more holes in the dirt. He knelt and dug with his hands.

Someplace on the Arney grounds, people

argued. Both twins listened tensely, while they recalled the hot, scratchy sweaters which had been thrown over their heads. "Are they coming this way?" Merry whispered.

"I don't think so," Terry whispered back. Suddenly he realized they could not be overheard. He grinned a little sheepishly. He turned his back to Merry and tapped on the wall, close to the floor. "Find my feet, Toby," he ordered.

They heard Toby bark in the excited, dog-talking way that meant, "Oh, *now* I know what you want!" They heard scratching sounds outside the wall.

"He's doing it!" Merry said.

"Keep tapping while I dig," Terry told Merry. He set to work harder than ever, now that he had outside help.

After a while Merry returned to dig with Terry, since just the sound of their voices kept Toby at work. "I'm glad Toby is big and strong," Merry said when she stopped to rest.

At just that minute she saw a slight shiver of dirt in the bottom of the pit they were digging beside the wall. Then a tiny hole broke in the bottom. Dirt sifted down, shaping a funnel of dirt.

Merry and Terry joined hands. They bounced around the floor of the old bathhouse in a made-up dance.

Suddenly a woolly head pushed through the hole in the floor. Toby struggled in. He stood in the middle of the floor to shake dirt from his heavy fur. Then he hung out his long tongue and tilted his head to peer out from under the shaggy hair that covered his eyes.

Merry and Terry hugged, petted, and cooed over their dog. Then they ran to the hole he had dug.

"It's big enough for us to crawl out, if Toby could crawl in!" Merry spoke loudly to convince herself that she would dare crawl under the bathhouse wall.

"I'll go first," Terry offered. "Then if our tunnel needs more digging, I can do it."

Merry sat on the floor and hugged Toby. Terry lay flat on the floor and started wriggling under the two-by-four. "Be careful, Terry," she begged. "You might get dirt in your nose."

"I'm all right," Terry answered.

Merry shivered with worry, while inch by inch Terry's sturdy body disappeared. Suddenly his feet slid out with a rush. "Come on, you can make it," he said from outside the wall.

Terry's shoulders were wider than Merry's, so she had less trouble crawling under the wall. Soon the twins stood close together with their faces tilted into the sunlight. Merry saw that Terry's dark lashes were wet. She did not try to swallow the tears that oozed down her hot cheeks.

"Stop bawling. Your face is dirty and you're making streaks," Terry said a little sharply to keep from crying, too.

Toby crawled through the hole and was petted again by both twins. Then they hurried down the path, away from the Arney house and the trouble they did not understand.

They saw Tina building sand castles on the beach with Tom and Penny. "They must be all right," Merry said, relieved that the rest of the Tuckers had not been touched by danger.

The path circled a clump of willows and brush.

Unexpectedly the twins came upon the old brown horse with Butch on its back.

"I saw that horse tied by the bathhouse!" Terry yelled. "I knew I'd find you, Butch Smith! I've got some things to say to you!"

From his high perch, Butch looked down at the excited twins. His face became as blank as a rag doll's. "Uh, I don't know what you're talking about," he managed to say.

By this time Tina and the younger Tuckers had heard the commotion. They scrambled around the willows and stared in amazement at the twins, Butch, and the old brown horse.

Merry pointed up at Butch. She yelled to Tina, "I don't know why, except maybe for the rickermeracker tracks, but Butch locked us up in Arneys' bathhouse. And Toby found our feet!"

"Aw, he couldn't capture both of us," Terry said disdainfully. "Somebody helped him lock us up!"

"Start at the beginning," Tina begged.

Merry explained about breaking the floor and digging their way out with Toby's help. "And it's all Butch's fault!" she finished stormily.

"I still don't know what you're blaming me for," Butch insisted. He looked nervously toward the Arney house.

"Somebody is living in the Arney house!" Terry shouted. "And stealing milk and—"

"Don't forget about the gas," Merry prompted.

"Somebody stole our picnic," Tom added. Sadly he looked at the old brown horse as if he would have liked to have been friends. He planted his feet wide apart, ready to fight. "And your horse broke our sun clock."

"We know it was you!" Terry shouted. "There are hoof marks all along the path. One horseshoe has a nick in it, and there is the nick!" He pointed at the prints the old brown horse had just made in the path. The prints were like those they had been seeing for days.

Butch looked as if he had been slapped. "I'm not a th-thief," he stammered.

"We don't want to think so, but you are the only new person around," Tina explained. "Nothing like this ever happened before you came."

Butch looked again toward the Arney house.

Then he told the circle of angry Tuckers, "If you know what's good for you, you'll just go home and mind your own business!" He poked his heels in the old horse's ribs and started down the path. He called back, "I thought the Tuckers were my friends!"

After a little silence Tina said worriedly, "I think Butch was crying."

"So do I," Merry agreed.

"Why should we care, after all the things he's done to us?" Terry demanded. With angry embarrassment he kicked a small stone out of the path.

"But, Terry, we don't know he did even one of those things," Tina reminded him.

"He didn't *say* he didn't!" Terry insisted.

Tom was the youngest of the Tuckers, but he had the kind of a mind that could handle a problem. "Butch must have been pretty busy to do all those things," he said.

"Well, somebody did," Terry said then, scowling uncertainly. Now that Tom had made it clear that one person would have found it hard to stay in the middle of the mystery, Terry wished he had not spoken so hastily to Butch. He had wanted Butch for a friend.

Penny moved close to Terry and put her hand in his. "Anyway, Tom found the oar, and that's what we came for."

Terry's fingers tightened on his sister's small hand. "Swell," he managed to mutter when he could no longer hear the clip-clop of Butch's horse's feet. "Where did he find it?"

"On the beach by the willows," Tom said. "And I'm going to carry it all the way home!"

"If you get tired, just let me know," Terry said.

But Terry's mind was not on the oar they had hunted for so many days. He was trying to figure out where Butch had gone. If Butch followed the shore path, he could be seen or heard once in the while. If he had hidden in the bushes, there would be broken twigs to show where he had left the path. Excepting for walks and paths leading from the beach to cottages, the road to the deserted farm was the only trail to leave the shore path. Nobody had lived on the farm for years and years. "Whillikers!" Terry muttered.

The Tuckers turned toward Grandpa's cottage with a sad-glad feeling. They had found the oar. They had escaped from the bathhouse.

But had they lost a friend?

14

A Mystery-Puzzle

As they walked the shore path the Tuckers stayed in shade as much as possible. The sun was high and hot.

Excitedly the twins repeated the story of their bathhouse adventure.

"We have to tell Dad and Grandpa about the things that have happened," Tina said positively. "You could have been hurt, so that makes it grownup business."

She thought about the parts of her puzzle. She pushed them around in her mind like moving the pieces of a jigsaw puzzle.

First, somebody had flipped pebbles at Grandma. A blond boy most certainly had been up in the cottonwood, since Tina had seen him with her own eyes. Almost at once Butch had appeared on the boat dock. If Butch had been up in the tree, how had he managed to cross the beach to the dock without being seen?

Next, a boy had burned cartons on the beach. He had not wanted to be seen. He had looked like Butch. Where had he found those cartons, and why had he collected them? Merry had lost no cartons. Why had the boy hidden?

Then there was the Arney house. Butch had walked back in that direction after their adventure when they lost the oar. Later, while sailing with Grandpa, Butch had been uneasy when he saw the house. The house was definitely being lived in by somebody who had no business there.

And there were no Smiths on the shore.

The trail was cut with a horse's hoofprints which led to the Arney house. It was the horse that connected Butch to the breaking of the sundial, the stolen food, and the twins' capture. The old brown horse had been near the Arney bathhouse, where the twins were captured and had escaped with Toby's help. The old brown horse evidently belonged to Butch.

Somebody had stolen gas. As Merry had pointed out, Butch had feet big enough to match the prints in the sand leading to and from the Tub. On the other hand, Butch was afraid of a boat. So why would he steal gas which had been mixed with oil for use in an outboard?

Somebody had dived and set the Arneys' red boat afloat to beat its bottom on shore. Somebody had broken into the boat storage room at the Arney house. Somebody had fished. Somebody had stolen milk.

Toby must be used to the horse. Toby had not raised an uproar about the old brown horse, either the night the skunk ate Terry's lunch, or today when Butch rode down the path.

Oh, Tina thought dismally. No matter how she arranged the pieces of the mystery-puzzle, she always came back to Butch and that brown horse.

Tina did not want Butch to be guilty. Butch was homely and lonely-acting, like a stray pup. But surely he would not steal or break into people's houses.

At once Tina saw in her mind a lost pup, with

big ears and solemn eyes. She had to admit that a pup would tip over garbage cans, sneak food from back porches, and sleep wherever it could find an open door.

"Butch isn't a pup!" Tina reminded herself sharply. "He's a boy!"

Just the same, the picture of the lonely stray pup would not leave her mind. All the way home she had the feeling that she had not yet found the piece of her puzzle which would fit all the other pieces together.

Penny nudged Tina's arm. "Tina," she said, "we're home, and you haven't said a word for miles and miles."

"We didn't walk miles and miles," Tom told Penny. But he, too, looked reproachfully at Tina.

"I was thinking," Tina said.

"That's what I figured," Tom said soberly. "So what did you decide? Did Butch lock up Terry and Merry?"

"How could he?" Terry argued. "There was just one of him and two of us."

"But you *yelled* at him, Terry," Tom reminded him. "You *said* he locked you up."

Terry punched the path with the toe of a sneaker. “Maybe I opened my trap too soon,” he admitted.

As they came in sight of Grandpa’s cottage, Merry tried to brush dirt from her shorts and T shirt. She spread her hands and made a face. “I’m a mess,” she told Tina. “Mother is going to want to know how we got so dirty.”

“And Grandpa will want to know where we found the oar,” Tom said. He shifted the oar to his left shoulder. His face was red, and his forehead was damp. He had carried the oar every step of the way.

"We'll tell them, of course," Tina said.

"When they find out what's been going on, they may tell us to stay home and mind our own business," Terry said.

"That's what Butch said, too," Tom told them.

"Probably Butch is right!" Merry said with an impish grin. Just seeing Grandpa's cottage made her feel better. "Let's forget about Butch. I'm hungry!"

"I see Grandma," Tom announced. "She has that funny hat on. I think she is throwing crumbs to the birds."

Terry loped ahead. "Hey, Grandma!" he shouted. "Save some of those bread crumbs for me. I'm starved!"

"I thought you would be," Grandma called across the cottage yard. "I baked cupcakes. Your mother is icing them right this minute."

"Dibs on licking the pan!" Tom yelled. He tried to run, but the long oar swung into the bushes.

"I see you found the oar!"

A voice seemed to come out of the sky. The Tuckers stopped in their tracks and looked up.

Penny was first to see Father's hand reach over the edge of the highest gable of the cottage. He was painting the wooden trim that outlined the eaves.

"Hi," Penny called. Anxiously she watched the paintbrush move high above the ground. "You'll be careful, won't you?" she asked.

"It's *my* neck I'm protecting," Father answered with a chuckle. "I'll be careful."

Grandpa came around the corner of the house. He wore no shirt. The long bill of his paint cap shaded the back of his wrinkled neck. He carried a ladder and a bucket with a brush sticking in the paint. Carefully he set the ladder below the window in the gable.

"Blow me down, so you found my oar! That's good." Grandpa winked at Tom, then started to climb the ladder. "How about you mateys checking in with Grandma? I heard something about a fish-fry on the beach when we finish the painting."

Merry bounced with indecision. She wanted to burst out with the story of being locked up and escaping from the Arneys' old bathhouse. At the same time she wanted freedom to explore until the mystery about Butch and the Arney house was cleared up.

The bright new paint on the cottage reminded her that the Fourth of July was only two days away. There was much to be done to finish arrangements for the floating fire party. Oh, this was a busy summer!

Tina seemed to read Merry's mind. "Has the mail come?" she asked Mother when Mother joined Grandma on the back steps.

"Yes, Tina," Mother answered, looking puzzled. "I don't understand it. You and Merry got eighteen letters. You even got a letter from the milkman!"

Tina and Merry clapped hands over their mouths to hold back giggles.

"I'll meet you in the trailer," Merry told Tina. She asked Mother, "Where did you put our letters?"

"On the table by the tray of cupcakes," Mother told her.

A few minutes later Merry joined Tina in the vacation trailer. She dropped the letters on her bunk. She gave Tina a plate of cupcakes and darted across the yard again. Almost at once, she returned with a carton of milk and two glasses. "Now," she declared with sparkling eyes, "let's lock the door and open our mail!"

Tina arranged their food on the tiny drop-leaf table under the window at the end of the trailer. She sat down and faced Merry across the table. Tina crossed fingers while Merry tore open the top letter in the stack.

"Why are you crossing your fingers?" Merry asked with surprise.

"I just had an awful thought," Tina said solemnly. "Suppose nobody wants to come to our floating fire party?"

"Oh-h," Merry wailed. Hastily she pulled out a sheet of note paper and pushed it at Tina. "You read it, Tina. If it says No I'll just die!"

Tina skimmed the words on the page and looked at the signature. "Mr. Wilson says he'll be happy to come," Tina said with a sigh of relief. "And he says don't worry about dessert, because he is bringing lots of ice cream."

"Goody!" Merry cried. She read the second

note. "Mrs. Corbett thinks our party is a good idea and is bringing a potato salad," she announced happily. "If Mrs. Corbett wants to come, so will everybody else."

Tina grinned back at Merry. Mrs. Corbett, one of their Yorkville neighbors, had not always been on the best of terms with the Tuckers.

When the last letter was read Merry and Tina held hands across the small table. "They're coming, Tina!" Merry cried. "Everybody is coming to our party."

"And," Tina said practically, "they are all planning to bring enough food to feed the Navy!"

"We told them it was a potluck party," Merry reminded her. "How could we keep it secret from Grandma and Mother if they had to cook all day?"

"Or from Father and Grandpa, if they had to pay the bills!" Tina finished with a giggle. She picked up the letters and arranged a neat stack. "Now where will we hide these letters?" she asked. "If we burn them, Mother will be curious. We can't put them in the garbage. One might fall out of the can."

"Give them to me," Merry said, bouncing up. "I'll hide them under my mattress!"

When Merry and Tina left the trailer they tried to act as if it were normal for them to receive eighteen letters in one day. But every time they looked at each other they burst into giggles.

"What's up?" Terry wanted to know. He rose from the back porch steps and looked accusingly at Merry.

Behind her hand Merry whispered, "Everybody is coming to the you-know-what party on the Fourth!"

"Hey, that's swell!" Terry said, but he did not smile. "I've been listening to the radio. The weatherman says it's going to rain on the Fourth."

"Oh, no!" Merry cried. "What'll we do with all the people? And how will we light our floating fires?"

Terry shrugged. "Search me. I just told you what he said."

Anxiously Tina studied the sky. For days it had been hot. Now a few clouds drifted in the sky, down where the Blue River drained Lake Annabelle. "Maybe those aren't storm clouds," she said hopefully.

Solemnly Tina, Merry, and Terry faced each other and crossed fingers on both hands. With a giggle Merry swung her right foot across her left. Terry gave a whoop of laughter and crossed his blue eyes. "There!" Terry declared. "We have everything so crossed up, it *can't* rain on the Fourth!"

Tom opened the kitchen screen door and stuck his head out. "Grandma says if we're rested enough she wants us to go fishing."

"Ready!" Terry, Tina, and Merry shouted together.

In the kitchen Grandma gave each of the Tuckers a wooden reel wound with a fish line. "We're going to have a fish-fry tonight on the beach," she told them. With a twinkle she added, "If you children catch some fish to fry!"

"How many fish shall we catch?" Tom asked soberly.

"All you can pull in," Mother told him cheerfully. "You are all to wear your life jackets. Tina, will you please stay on the boat dock with Tom and Penny? You twins may go out about fifty yards from shore in the Tub. Grandma will work in the kitchen. By the time she is finished, the men should have the painting done. Father will clean the fish. I'll run all the beach errands and light the charcoal grill to have the coals white-hot. Well?" Mother looked around the circle. "Have I left out anything?"

"Sounds like a neat plan," Terry said, nodding his head. "Come on, Tom. Help me dig worms."

"Ugh," Merry said, and wrinkled her nose.

"You did forget the worms, Mother!"

Fishing was a summertime sport enjoyed by all the Tuckers. In a few minutes Tina followed Tom and Penny onto the boat dock. She watched the twins row the heavy Tub out to a spot they called the "fishin' hole."

Tom chose the right side of the dock where he could watch Mother set the table and light the fire in the grill.

Penny chose the left side with its view of the shore path leading to the Arney house. Secretly she hoped for a glimpse of Butch and the old brown horse.

Tina dropped her jerkline off the end of the dock into the deep water near the old stove Grandpa used to hold the dock in place. She watched the twins point and shift the Tub. When they agreed on a fishing spot, Terry dropped the anchor overboard. Merry squealed when she baited her hook. Then nobody talked. Tina could hear the rustle of leaves, the slight swish of still water, and the early evening birdcalls. The odor of pineapple and hot chocolate drifted down from the cottage. Next door somebody was frying a steak. The good smell made Tina's mouth water so much, she could barely wait for a fish to swallow the worm on her hook.

"Got one!" Tom declared. Hand over hand he began to pull up his line, dropping it in neat coils on the dock. When he lifted a perch from the water he held it up for Terry to see. "Big enough to keep?" he called, filled with pride, but trying not to sound conceited.

"Looks good to me," Terry shouted back. "Oops! I have a fish!"

"Me, too!" Merry shouted.

Penny was next to feel the heavy tug of a biting fish. She tangled her line around her feet and refused to touch the fish she caught. Tina left her own line to help Penny. By the time she returned to the end of the dock, a fish had eaten her bait without getting hooked. She rebaited and tossed out her line. Contentedly she let her eyes follow the shoreline path to the faraway red dot that was the Arney house.

She puckered her brows. Was that a boat leaving the dock at the Arney house? The low rays of the sun glistened on something red. The red spot moved. Tina squinted, trying to follow the red spot, but was interrupted by a tug on her fish-line. When she had brought in her perch and rebaited her hook, she looked at the lake again. Several fishing boats sat on the blue water. A sailboat flapped its canvas and waited for wind. In the distance a speedboat pulled a water skier. But she did not see the red boat which belonged to Todd Arney.

After the long walk to the Arney house, the Tuckers welcomed the lazy quiet of fishing. They called to each other, keeping track of the number of perch each had caught. Once in the while there was a disappointed, "Oh!" when a fish got away, or an excited squeal when an especially fat perch was pulled in.

Up at the cottage Father gave a war whoop and yelled, "Work's all done. Now I can throw away my paintbrush!"

Cheerfully Grandpa called, "If you have enough energy left to yell, you can just come around here and help me finish this window, Bill Tucker!"

"Sure thing!" Father answered.

Suddenly Tina straightened. A red boat was coming down the lake—fast! And something was wrong. There seemed to be three people in the boat, and some kind of struggle was going on.

On came the boat, straight toward the Tuckers' dock. When it did not slow up, Tina hurried Penny and Tom to the end near shore where the water was shallow. Just as they reached the ramp connecting the dock with the shore, the red boat cut a sharp turnabout. Water rolled over the dock. A frightened glance told Tina one of the three in the boat was Butch. He was clinging to the side of the boat with both hands. Each time the boat rocked, his head jerked.

"The twins, Bill!" Mother shrieked.

15

Fun—for Nobody!

"The twins, Bill!" Mother screamed again. "Their boat will be hit!"

Father dropped his paintbrush and ran. "Terry," he yelled, "get that anchor up, quick!"

Tina had been so worried about Penny and Tom, she had not realized that Terry and Merry might be in danger. Now she saw that the red Arney boat was cutting circles around the Tub, which was anchored in one spot.

Sturdily Terry pulled at the anchor, while Merry held his belt to help him balance. Both twins wore life preservers. But Tina knew those preservers were not enough protection should the twins be knocked out of the Tub. The careening red boat could ram them with its bow or knock them unconscious with a sideswipe. Worst of all, their arms and legs could be cut by propeller blades.

"Merry, Terry," Tina whispered prayerfully as she watched them pull up the anchor.

She heard feet pound down the trail just as Terry heaved up the anchor.

"Sit down in the middle of the boat, mateys!" Grandpa roared with such authority Tina relaxed enough to look from the twins to the Arney boat.

In the boat with Butch were the two teenagers who had kicked down the sundial.

How they fitted into her mystery-puzzle, she did not know.

The dark boy Terry called Muscle Man was steering Todd Arney's boat and yelling like a maniac. Both Blondy and Butch clung to the sides of the boat. Butch was too frightened to make a sound. Blondy was bawling at Muscle Man, "Stop it, you crazy goon! What are you trying to do, drown all of us?"

"Fun, man, fun!" Muscle Man whooped.

Crazed with excitement, he circled the Tub again.

"I'll call the sheriff," Father told Grandpa. He left the dock on the run.

This time the red boat slid on its own wake. It hit the Tub broadside.

Tina clenched her fists, almost afraid to look. Then she saw that Grandpa's sturdy boat simply moved across the surface of the water. The twins huddled together in the bottom of the boat.

The red boat did not fare so well. It tipped crazily. Muscle Man did not know how to pull back on course. The red boat wobbled and lurched. It barely missed the boat dock and headed for the Tub again. Grandpa roared, but there was nothing he could do. His motor was on its rack on the dock. The twins could not sit on floorboards and row.

This time the red boat hit the Tub on its flat stern. The Tub moved forward. Muscle Man spun the wheel enough to sideswipe the Tub. By this time the water was so stirred up, both boats rocked dangerously.

Butch's nerve broke. He stood up in the swaying boat and screamed, "Terry! I didn't steal! *They* did!"

Blondy lunged toward Butch, and so did Muscle Man. Terrified, Butch threw up both hands to protect his head. The red boat swerved. Butch fell headfirst into the water, at the mercy of sharp, whirring propellers and smashing boats.

"*Give the boy a chance!*" Grandpa roared.

For a second Muscle Man hesitated. Then he turned the red boat and hit the dock, missing Butch. Like a wild animal running for shelter, the boat slid high and dry on the canvas surface of the dock. Blondy was flung into the water. Muscle Man landed on the dock. He tried to get up, then collapsed. Blondy climbed to the dock and sat with his head on his folded arms.

Tina saw Butch's arms thrash water near the Tub, then he sank.

Grandpa had not yet cleaned up after painting. He wore no shirt. Hastily he stripped off shoes and socks and dived. He swam toward Butch.

Now that the red boat was no longer a menace,

Terry stood up in the Tub. He took off his shirt and tied it firmly to the end of an oar. When Butch came to the surface, Terry swung the oar. A sleeve landed within inches of Butch's clawing hands.

With all his strength Terry raised the shirt, now wet, and whipped it to Butch. Butch's head sank, but so did the shirt.

"Pull, Terry!" Merry screamed. "Butch is hanging on!"

Hand over hand the twins pulled in the oar, dragging Butch who had a drowning man's grip on the shirt sleeve. When Butch was in arm's reach, Terry fastened both hands in Butch's white hair. Merry braced the oar, since Butch still clung to the shirt.

"I've got him," Terry panted.

"Keep his mouth and nose out of water, Terry," Mother called from shore where she and Grandma stood with arms around each other.

Grandpa reached the Tub. He bounced on water and pulled himself into the boat. The Tub tipped till its wooden rim scooped water. Grandpa lifted Butch into the boat, laid him over a seat

and rowed swiftly back to the dock.

Penny was first of the Tuckers to go near the tall boys. She stooped over Muscle Man. "You should have Grandpa teach you about boats," she said soberly. Gently she laid her hand on his forehead. "Do you feel sick?" she asked.

"Aw, g'way, kid," Muscle Man growled. He tried to roll away from Penny.

"She's just trying to help," Blondy said.

Tina and Mother hurried to help Grandpa lift Butch onto the dock. There Grandpa worked water from Butch's lungs. Grandma wrapped him in a blanket. Mother felt the twins' bones and kissed the top of Grandpa's head. Then she hurried to the house for the hot chocolate Grandma had made.

Father carried the chocolate pot and cups for Mother and walked over to the boys who sat close together with heads on arms. "Are you boys O.K.?" he asked.

"We'll live," Muscle Man snapped.

"Then perhaps you'd like to explain why you pulled this crazy stunt," Dad said sternly.

"We ain't talkin'," Muscle Man declared.

In a very short time Butch sat up and smiled weakly at the Tuckers. "Thanks," he said shakily. Then he edged away from Muscle Man.

"Take it easy, matey," Grandpa told Butch. "Nobody is going to hurt you."

Tina saw that Butch was not convinced. But when his head quit spinning, he climbed into the Tub. He patted its strong wooden seat and ran his fingers over its ribbing. "Good old boat," he said. From the look on Butch's face, Tina sensed that Butch no longer feared boats and water. He had survived both.

Soberly, Tom walked around the Arneys' ruined boat. "Poor boat," he said.

When the sheriff arrived, Muscle Man and Blondy answered his questions with grunts. It was soon clear they were runaways from Chicago. They had broken into the Arney house. When they had used up the Arneys' supplies, they stole the things they needed.

"Milk?" Terry asked.

Merry looked at Muscle Man's big feet. "Gas?" she asked.

"Our picnic?" Tom wanted to know.

"Sure, sure," Muscle Man said, shrugging. "We gotta live, don't we?"

"Did you ever try working for a living?" the sheriff asked drily. He was a tall, uniformed man with a thin, alert face.

Reproachfully Terry turned on Butch. "Why didn't you tell us you weren't a thief?"

"You thought I was, so you wouldn't have believed me," Butch said. Tears welled in his gray eyes.

The sheriff glanced sharply at Butch when Grandpa told the story of the accident. "How did you happen to be in the boat?" he asked Butch.

"They put me in and held me," Butch said.

"Why?"

Muscle Man looked at Blondy who shrugged and said, "Go ahead, tell him. We're caught."

"He was ridin' that old brown horse to town to squeal on us," Muscle Man said angrily. "I decided to scare him so he wouldn't dare open his trap."

As the sheriff asked questions, the story came out. Butch had seen the boys break into the Arney house. They pulled him from his horse. Muscle

Man beat him up. Butch had looked so stubborn they followed him home. They stole the horse to keep Butch from getting in touch with the law. When they raided cottages for supplies, they rode the horse. Usually Blondy stood watch while Muscle Man took what he wanted. For two weeks there had been a constant struggle between Butch and the runaways. Each time they stole his horse, Butch found it again and took it home.

Since Butch had known the Tuckers, he had been hiding his horse in the woods above the beach.

"So that's why Toby didn't bark!" Tina burst out. "He thought the horse belonged there!"

"You mateys seem to know a lot about this," Grandpa said with a questioning look at Tina.

All their worries and suspicions tumbled out as Terry, Merry, and Tina told why they had connected Butch with thievery and trespassing. "It was because of the horse," Tina told Butch apologetically. "His hoofprints were on the paths. You were the only one we had ever seen ride him."

"We're sorry," Merry said earnestly. "We didn't *want* to think you would steal."

"I even thought your family was living in the Arney house," Terry confessed.

Butch's eyes flashed. "If you knew my pop, you wouldn't say that!" He stood up and tightened the belt on his dripping clothes. "I have to go now. My Mom will be worried sick."

"Let me take you," Father offered.

"Uh, n-no, thanks," Butch stammered. "I'll ride my horse."

"Not until you put on dry clothes and have something to eat," Mother said firmly.

The sheriff shook hands with Father and Grandpa. Then he said firmly, "Come on, fellows. Your vacation is over."

Muscle Man had trouble getting to his feet. Anxiously Penny asked, "Is he hurt?"

"I'll have a doctor check him," the sheriff told Penny. "Then I'll call his father to come to Yorkville. He will have some bills to pay."

"You're in trouble, aren't you?" Tom asked soberly.

"What's it to you?" Muscle Man snapped.

"You've got everything. Folks, good food, and a lake to play in. I ain't got nothin'!"

"I'm sorry," Penny said earnestly.

"Aw," Muscle Man grunted and stamped up the trail to the sheriff's car in the parking lot.

Just as the sheriff gestured for the boys to climb into his car, Merry darted forward. "You locked Terry and me in the bathhouse!" she accused.

"Well?" Muscle Man asked, determined to be tough to the end. "You was snoopin', wasn't you?"

The minute the sheriff's car left the parking lot, Father turned to the twins. "Out with it," he ordered. "What's this about getting locked up?"

While the twins told how Toby had "found their feet," Tina puzzled over the jigsaw pieces she had been arranging in her mind. "I put all the pieces in the wrong places," she thought.

But the mystery was not completely solved. Why didn't Butch want the Tuckers to know where he lived? Who had thrown pebbles at Grandma? Who had burned cartons?

Tina's thoughts were interrupted by a sharp question from Father. "Are you sure all the secrets are out in the open? What about those milk cartons? Do they have anything to do with this Arney mess?"

"Oh, no!" Merry said earnestly. "The cartons are a secret, but a nice one. Cross my heart!"

Father walked between the twins. Tina noticed that he studied the face of each of his children in turn. His expression seemed to say, "How did all of this happen without my knowing about it?" He raised his eyebrow at Grandpa and said, "Why parents get gray!"

"Blow me down, I'm starved!" Grandpa rumbled. "Bill, if you will finish that window for me, I'll change into dry clothes and clean the fish."

"Can't the window wait?" Grandma asked.

Grandpa squinted at the sky, where the last rays of sun struck clouds. "Looks like rain," he decided.

"Oh, no!" Merry moaned. "It can't rain on the Fourth of July."

Grandpa could clean fish faster than anybody

on Lake Annabelle. In a very short time the Tuckers stood in a hungry circle to watch Grandma fry fish.

It was dark when they gathered around the beach table, but the lanterns overhead cast friendly circles of light. Butch wore Terry's clothes and spoke only when he was spoken to. He fidgeted when he glanced at the woods above the beach. From Grandpa to Tom, the Tuckers tried to set him at ease.

Butch was not used to so much attention. He began every sentence with an "uh." Finally he choked on a fish bone and asked to be excused. Terry went with Butch to be sure he was all right, but he returned to the table alone.

"Where's Butch?" Mother asked.

Terry shrugged and flung out his hands. "One minute he was right there beside me. And the next, he was gone."

"Well, that beats all!" Merry said, duplicating Grandpa's words and tone so exactly everybody laughed.

"Did Butch tell you where he lives?" Penny asked anxiously.

"How could he?" Tom demanded. "He had a fish bone in his throat."

"He got the bone out," Terry said. "But why did he disappear?"

16
The Smiths at Last

The next morning Grandma directed a brisk clearing of the breakfast table. Then she carried her largest mixing bowl to the table. Every Fourth of July she baked a huge flat cake and decorated it with red, white, and blue icing.

Merry's mouth watered when she thought about Grandma's cake and Mr. Wilson's ice cream. The party! Day after tomorrow was the Fourth.

She shaped the words "You-know-what!" without making a sound. Tina and Terry raced with her to the shed to count milk cartons.

"Enough!" Merry declared.

Terry hitched up his belt. "Good!" he said. "I

didn't plan to collect any more cartons. I am going to find Butch Smith today if it takes me till midnight." He didn't look at his sisters when he added, "Butch must think I'm an awful stinker. Making rickermeracker tracks to scare him, and accusing him of stealing."

"He doesn't know about the tracks," Merry said to comfort Terry.

"That horse by the bathhouse is the clue," Tina said, thinking of her mystery-puzzle. "We can follow his tracks." Merry gasped, and Tina promised quickly, "We won't go near the bathhouse."

Usually the five Tuckers swam when their morning work was done. But today they hurried along the shore path to the old road. Then they followed the hoofprints up the road. Toby sniffed at the newest tracks.

At a turn in the old road the Tuckers had their first view of the old farm. Terry puckered his brows. The fences seemed straighter than he remembered. There were two cows in a pasture. They wore bells that rang with a sleepy-sounding *clung-clong*.

"Are you sure nobody lives on that farm?" Tina asked Terry. "I see green rows in a garden near the back porch."

"And *I* see smoke coming out of the chimney!" Tom declared.

Merry ran down the road. "Come on," she invited. "I want a drink of water."

"Me, too," Tom said loudly. He trotted at Merry's heels.

The road wound through a woods thick with underbrush. Suddenly it entered an open field near some old sheds and a barn. A gate closed the road.

"Shall we climb over?" Merry asked Terry.

"Sure," Terry answered. "We won't get a drink of water if we stay on this side of the gate."

A little hesitantly the Tuckers climbed the gate and walked toward the old house.

"Are we trespassing?" Merry asked Tina.

"Well, we're not sneaking like Muscle Man and Blondy," Tina explained, "so we're visiting instead of trespassing."

"That's good," Tom said. "'Cause I see the man we're visiting."

Tom pointed to a tall man who was chopping wood near the back steps. While he swung the ax, the man balanced against a porch step. Each time he made a cut in the wood, he pushed himself into position and wiped his face.

"The man has a big white leg," Tom said solemnly.

"That's a cast," Tina said in a low voice. "He must have a broken leg."

Slowly they walked forward. None of the Tuckers knew what to say to the man who worked with a cast on his leg.

Tom stepped on a piece of dry wood. The man heard the small noise and turned around. With one hand on Toby's collar, Tom said, "You look just like Butch."

"I'm Butch's father," the man answered in a cheerful but tired voice. "And you must be the Tuckers. Butch mentioned twins."

"Butch didn't tell us about you," Tom said.

Hastily Tina cut in to change the subject. "May we have a drink of water?"

"Help yourself," Mr. Smith invited. He waved at the pump on the porch. "If you will excuse me,

I'll just go ahead with this wood chopping while I have the hang of it."

While Terry filled a tin cup for each in turn, beginning with Tom, the Tuckers tried not to stare at Butch's father.

The man was tall and thin. He looked exactly like a grown-up Butch. He had white hair, eyebrows, and lashes, and pale gray eyes. His skin, too, was as white as Butch's had been when they first met him. When Mr. Smith swung the ax, his face turned red.

"You shouldn't be doing that," Tina said with concern.

"Have to," Mr. Smith panted. "We have no electricity yet, and we need the wood for cooking."

"Let me do it for you," Terry offered. He stepped forward and reached for the ax, but Mr. Smith waved him back.

"As long as I have one leg to stand on, no kid does my work for me." Mr. Smith smiled at his own joke, but he looked so tired and weak that Penny gave him her cup of water.

"Thank you, Penny," he said.

"How do you know my name?" she asked with surprise.

"You're the youngest Tucker girl, so that makes you Penny," Mr. Smith explained. "I've heard so much about all of you in the past couple of weeks, I can tell you what color your bathing suits are and what you like for breakfast."

A white-haired boy came around the corner, then ducked back. Tina had time to recognize the boy who had flipped pebbles at Grandma. Later the same boy had burned cartons to cook fish.

"That's Dutch," Merry whispered impishly, reminding Tina of the make-believe twin Father

had described the day Terry met Butch.

"Ssh," Tina warned.

"Come here, Mel," Mr. Smith called. "We have company."

Shyly the boy came around the corner. "This is Melvin," Mr. Smith said. "He is carrying water to his mother's garden."

Tina thought he looked too small to carry two buckets. Water splashed on his bare feet when he hurried around the corner again.

"Where's Butch?" Tom asked.

"He is working in the barn," Mr. Smith told him.

Tina, Merry, Tom, and Penny followed Terry, who remembered where to find the barn.

They found Butch cleaning a tumbledown stall. When Terry spoke to him, Butch rubbed his hands on his jeans. He did not seem to know what to say.

"We met your father and brother," Merry told Butch.

"They're nice," Tom said.

"It takes nerve to work with that cast on," Terry said.

Butch looked pleased. "Pop's great, isn't he?"

"Why didn't you tell us where you lived?" Tina asked.

Butch scraped the ground with one bare foot and hung his head. "Uh," he said, "I didn't think you would want to be friends with a farm kid. I was so darned lonesome and in so much trouble with those guys, I couldn't take any chances. I had to see somebody once in the while."

Merry said sharply, "Uncle Fred is a farmer, and we like him."

"His farm is a big, fine one," Butch insisted, still looking at the ground.

Gently Tina told Butch, "Uncle Fred worked to make it big and fine. Yours can be a fine farm some day."

Butch's face lighted. "That's what Pop says!" he said with relief. "Say, would you like to meet my mom? She hasn't had company since we moved here."

Butch led the way to the little garden Tina had seen from the road. Mrs. Smith was hoeing vegetables. Mel was watering a row of new green rhubarb plants.

"So you're the Tuckers," Mrs. Smith said. "I've been wanting to thank you for being so kind to Rodney."

"To who?" Tom asked, looking around.

"Uh, that's me," Butch admitted. "Rodney Smith."

Soberly Tom looked at Butch while he got used to his name. Then he said with a wide grin, "Terry's name is Terrence!"

"Now that you know all of each other's secrets," Mrs. Smith said with a smile, "let's go sit in the shade and get acquainted."

Tina wondered if Mrs. Smith knew all the secrets connecting Butch with the runaways from Chicago. "All?" she asked in a low voice.

Mrs. Smith overheard Tina. She said quietly, "Yes, Tina, Butch has told us everything. We feel so indebted to you Tuckers—but how can we find words to thank you for saving Butch's life?"

The words were spoken so quietly Tina felt the same awe she felt in church on Easter morning. She felt herself surrounded by this family's love.

The bare, weedy yard was shaded by one large

maple. There the grass had been cut around an old cot. Butch helped his tired father to clump over the rough ground on crutches. The man sank onto the cot and wiped his face. "I simply must reduce," he said, trying to joke. "One leg is too fat."

Tina went with Mrs. Smith to the unpainted house with the cracked windows mended with brown tape. She looked around the shabby kitchen. It was clean enough to please Grandma. In one corner a woodbox held wood cut by the man with a cast.

Mrs. Smith glowed with the excitement of having company. While she arranged a plate of cookies and poured milk she told Tina, "We're from Chicago. I worked in a cafe and my husband ran a gas station. For years we dreamed of owning a farm. We didn't want our boys to grow up in a street gang. You can imagine how excited we were to move here. Then Bob stepped on a rotten board and broke his leg before our furniture was unloaded! I don't know what we'd have done without our boys. It broke my heart for Butch to be bullied by those young hoodlums

VITAMIN
MILK

when he was working so hard. But I was proud of him for having nerve enough to resist them."

Tina was glad Mrs. Smith did not glance up. She could feel her face burn with embarrassment for her own suspicions about Butch.

"Will you carry the glasses, Tina, please?" Mrs. Smith asked. "I'll carry the food."

When they returned to the group in the shade, Tina saw that Tom and Penny were getting acquainted with Mel. Mel looked puzzled every time Penny called him "Dutch."

While they ate, Butch told his story. Most of it Tina already knew from having listened to the sheriff's questions. She looked at Butch with real respect when she learned of the determined stand of one thin, lonely boy against the runaways.

At first the boys had forced Butch to provide milk from the farm.

"We didn't have enough to share," Butch explained, "so I quit. They tried to make me steal milk for them, but I wouldn't." He glanced at Mel and said, "Mel thought I did, so he collected the milk cartons he found on the beaches and along the paths and burned them."

Mel ducked his head. "Butch is working as hard as he can," Mel said loyally. "I couldn't let him get in trouble with the milkman."

"But why did you flip pebbles at Grandma?" Tina asked.

Mel wiggled his shoulders. "I'm sorry about that," he said. "I couldn't see who it was under the funny hat. I was trying to clear the beach so I could tell Butch our horse was gone again, and he'd have to walk home."

Merry had been listening. Suddenly she burst out, "Well, I don't see why you didn't invite all of us up here to help you. We'd have had fun."

"I know that now," Butch confessed. "But I had never lived in the country before. I didn't know anybody rich enough to own a house just for fun. I didn't think you'd want a farm kid around."

"Why!" Merry looked outraged. Then she giggled so hard she choked. "Rich! Us?" she gurgled. "Butch, did you ever see our station wagon?"

Each Tucker pictured Father's rattley old

blue station wagon and burst into laughter. "C-Come ride in our l-limousine sometime!" Tina giggled.

Quickly Merry added, "Day after tomorrow! Father will drive up and bring all of you to our floating fire party."

"Our what?" Tom asked.

"Oh!" Merry slapped her hand over her mouth. "I made Terry promise not to tell, and I'm telling." She hugged Tom and reminded him, "Tom, you know! Our secret. I call it floating fire."

Butch looked puzzled, but Tina, Terry, and Merry exchanged a secret glance. The mystery was cleared up, and they could look forward to their party without worry.

Tina stood up and thanked Mrs. Smith for the cookies and milk. She tried to think of some way to thank Butch for being the kind of boy he was, and not the kind she had suspected. All she could say was, "See you on the Fourth of July."

Terry, Merry, and Tom followed Tina, but Penny sank back into the grass beside Mel.

"Penny, don't get too far behind," Tina called

back. "You'd have to run to catch up, and that would make you cough."

"I'm going to cough anyway," Penny gasped.

The four Tuckers ran back to Penny.

"Oh, no, Penny!" Merry objected. "You can't be sick for the Fourth. You just can't!"

Tina tested Penny's forehead. "She's hot," Tina said. "We're a long way from home."

Tom held out his hands. "Terry and I could make a cradle with our hands and carry her," he said sturdily.

Butch left the yard on the run and Mrs. Smith smiled. "Butch has the answer to your problem," she promised.

In a few minutes Butch led the old brown horse into the yard. Mrs. Smith lifted Penny onto its bare back. Fearfully Penny fastened her small hands into its mane. "I'll fall off," Penny cried.

"Tina can ride and hold you on," Butch said to comfort Penny.

"I've never ridden a horse in my life!" Tina gasped.

"Then Mel can ride with Penny, and I'll lead," Butch said.

Tina noticed that Butch did not stammer now that he was no longer frightened.

The Tuckers, the Smith boys, the old brown horse, and Toby slowly crossed the farm, walked down the old road, and along the shore path. Tina walked on one side of the horse, and Merry on the other.

When they came to the spot where the brook flowed from the spring, Butch ducked into the bushes. Suddenly he grew eight feet tall. "The rickermeracker!" he called over their heads. "The rickermeracker is loose again!"

Terry looked sheepish. "I'm sorry about that," he confessed. "But you laughed at me!"

"That's all right," Butch said. "I found the stilts while I was hunting for my horse."

"So that's where my stilts and mitt went." Tom looked accusingly at Terry.

"So *I* have holes in my head and forget where I leave things," Terry retorted. "I found those stilts on the beach where *you* left them!"

"So you're all even," Merry interrupted, making peace.

The minute they reached home Mother put Penny to bed in the trailer. Grandma made up a big basket of food for the Smiths. When Butch could not balance the basket on the horse, Father and Grandpa took it to the farm in the station wagon. "Our limousine," Terry reminded Butch with a grin, when Father opened the door for Butch and Terry.

They returned three hours later, hungry, dirty, and pleased with themselves.

"I learned to milk!" Terry told Merry.

"I took over the woodpile," Father said.

"And I gave that garden a good hoeing before it rains," Grandpa said. "What's for supper?"

Merry ran to the window and peered at the

sky. On the far horizon where the Blue River drained Lake Annabelle, gray clouds rolled heavily.

"It can't rain for the Fourth!" she wailed.

17
Floating Fire

The rain started before dawn. Merry put both feet on the springs of the bunk over her head and pushed. Sleepily Tina stuck her head over the edge. "Tina," Merry moaned, "it's pouring!"

"Oh, no!" Tina mourned, but that did not stop the rain. It came down dismally, drearily, and endlessly.

All day the Tuckers stared at Lake Annabelle and watched their breath make steamy spots on the windows. A dozen times during the morning Tina, Merry, and Terry held secret meetings in corners. They put beach towels over their heads and ran to the shed to check the milk cartons so often they worried Tom and Penny. "Is our secret dry?" Tom wanted to know.

Dad carried Penny from the trailer to the davenport in the living room. The cat, Sugar, slept on her feet. Grandma made her favorite chicken soup. "I'll be well for tomorrow," Penny promised, but still Merry was not convinced. Penny looked hot and tired.

"She's been trying to keep up with the rest of you," Mother said worriedly.

Merry carried her violin to Grandma's bedroom. She practiced till Terry begged her to stop. "I have to practice for our you-know-what!" she insisted stubbornly.

"We'll need water wings for our I-know-what," Terry said sourly.

It was still raining when Merry and Tina put away the last of the lunch dishes. But Merry went to the edge of the kitchen porch. She held out her hand. "It's just sprinkling," she decided. "We have things to do."

"Well, bundle up," Mother agreed. "One sick child is more than enough."

When they were well away from the house, Merry started snatching leaves from the bushes.

"We haven't tested the current," she explained before she could be questioned. "We don't know where to put Grandpa's boat when we light our floating fires."

"Under an umbrella," Terry said with a scowl.

Indignantly Merry faced her twin. "I'm going to have our party," she cried, "even if I have to go out in the rain alone!"

With her hands full of leaves Merry led the parade down the beach path. Water poured through the sundial. Not a speck of shadow was cast to tell the time.

Terry steadied the boat while Merry and Tina climbed aboard. Then he rowed back and forth in front of the picnic table. Every few feet Merry dropped leaves on the water to see which way they floated. Rain splatted down and pushed the leaves in circles. Water ran down their faces. It dripped off noses and chins. Merry did not mind the rain, since nobody could know she was crying.

The sun broke through the clouds just in time to color the sky with a sunset. But that was too late to cheer the Tuckers. It had already been a ruined day as far as they were concerned.

In pajamas Tina, Merry, Terry, and Tom waited for Father to carry Penny to the trailer. They stood in a circle around Grandma's red, white, and blue cake. Tom heaped a big square of soda crackers with peanut butter. He returned to stare at the cake. "If it rains," he said, "we'll have all the cake we can eat."

"Oh, Tom!" Merry wailed and ran to bed.

On the morning of the Fourth of July, Merry was afraid to open her eyes. Stiffly she lay in her bunk and listened. Was that rain she heard? Cautiously she peeked. There stood Tina, look-

ing long-legged in her red knit pajamas. She was brushing her teeth.

With a radiant smile Tina cried, "The sun is shining!" She danced across the room.

Merry bounced. "We have things to do!"

Mother and Grandma were amazed at the speed with which dishes were washed, beds made, and clothing put away. In half their usual work time the Tuckers were on the beach.

Tom stopped at the sundial to straighten the hour pegs. Merry, Tina, and Terry worked in the picnic area. They carried wood and arranged a huge tepee in the firepit. Merry raked the sand till not a candy-bar wrapper remained. Out of sight of adults, Tom, Tina, and Terry carried benches and folding chairs from the shed. Toby ran till his long ears flopped and his tongue hung out. Sugar leaped out of the bushes when feet hurried past his hiding place.

Each time one of the Tuckers came within speaking distance, Penny begged, "Tell me what you are doing now!" Grownups looked puzzled when answers were whispered.

Merry asked urgently, "You aren't going to

need your boat today, are you, Grandpa?"

"Well-l, matey," Grandpa rumbled, "when you put it that way—no."

Soon after the arrival of Aunt Anne and Uncle Fred, every young Tucker, even Penny, disappeared. In a few minutes she returned to the cottage, riding on Terry's back. She looked pink and excited. "I helped," she announced happily. But not one question would Penny answer about the mysterious trips her brothers and sisters made across the back yard. From the shed to the beach they hurried with odd-looking bundles wrapped in their big beach towels.

When Grandma handed out dishes of food to be carried to the picnic table on the beach, Merry warned, "Just a minute, Grandma, till I see if we're ready." She returned in a few minutes. "O.K., we can eat now," she said.

"Well, this beats all!" Grandpa rumbled. "Since when do we tell Grandma when to serve her food?"

"Just today," Merry promised. As she picked up a bowl of baked beans, she kissed Grandma's ear. Merry raced ahead and directed the seating of the table. No grownup faced the Tub. It was heaped high with milk cartons and covered with bright beach towels.

No Tucker could concentrate on food while faced with that lumpy-bumpy, secret load in the Tub. Even Tom wandered away from the table before dessert. Grandpa shook his head. "I don't understand this. Something is wrong when Tom doesn't eat."

"Not wrong, Grandpa!" Merry said sunnily. "But just right! Father, isn't it time to go for the Smiths?"

"O.K." Father agreed. "Who wants to ride with me?"

"I!" shouted the Tuckers. Even Penny rode to the farm and back. She sat beside Mr. Smith and shielded his broken leg with all the care she was used to receiving when sick.

The children rushed Butch and Mel to the beach.

"Swim!" Terry shouted. "Last one in is a firecracker!" In a few minutes they were all in the water.

When they tired of swimming, Merry and

Tina shared a rubber raft and listened to the happy sounds coming from the beach. All the cottages were open for the holiday. People swam, picnicked, and boated. Water skiers sent up rooster-tails of spray behind fast boats. A few fishermen drifted toward the lonely wooded shore where Mel had burned the cartons. Portable radios blared marches and speeches. Firecrackers popped. People shouted. Dogs barked.

"Don't you just love the Fourth?" Merry sighed blissfully.

"I thought this day would never come," Tina answered.

The drone of a motor grew in volume. Suddenly their rubber raft rocked on the wake of a boat. The boat shot past before Tina gasped, "That was Jim Jackson!"

The boat turned in a wide circle. It went dead in the water well out of the way of their legs and arms.

"Swim over here," a teasing voice called. "We have something for you."

A few swift strokes carried the girls to the Jacksons' boat. Both Tina and Merry trod water while they grinned up at their favorite teen-ager, Jim Jackson, who lived next door in Yorkville.

"So you came to our party," Merry said, almost too happy to believe it.

"We wouldn't miss it," Mr. Jackson said good-naturedly. Mrs. Jackson rummaged and brought out two ice-cream bars. Jim handed them to Tina and Merry.

"What will we do with these?" Merry squealed, reaching up a dripping arm.

"You figure it out," Jim answered and laughed. He backed away from the girls, then sped toward Grandpa's dock.

"Wh-what—" Tina gasped, waving the cold treat.

"I'm going to float and eat mine," Merry declared. "Mmmm. Isn't this messy fun?"

"We'd better go in and get dressed," Tina urged.

Merry giggled. "I'll bet Grandma wonders what's happening."

The minute the last cold bite of ice cream was eaten, Merry and Tina swam to shore with the rubber raft. They dressed in the trailer, then ran to greet their guests whose cars were already filling the parking lot. Each family brought bathing suits and food. Merry swished her dark hair and danced on her toes as she ran from one guest to another.

"Surprise, surprise!" friends shouted to Grandma and Grandpa, Mother and Father. Grandma's cheeks were a pink contrast to her white hair as she told each guest, "I'm glad you came!"

Grandpa and Father tried to seat new arrivals, but found Terry, Tom, Butch, and Mel placing chairs. "You're company, too, Father," Tom said excitedly. "This party is our secret."

"Oh, it's a nice secret!" Mother said, hugging Merry who hurried to meet lake neighbors who had saved milk cartons.

Aunt Anne trotted at Merry's heels. "Jane Fields!" she cried. "Let me see that precious baby."

Merry felt so happy she began to hum. A voice started to sing in her ear, and it was Jim Jackson.

"Tina said you have a job for me tonight," he

said with a big broad smile.

"Meet us on the dock when the stars start coming out," Merry said. She skipped away, giggling at Jim's bewilderment.

Several guests came in boats. Swimmers splashed near the dock. The beach was dotted with sunbathers. Croquet, horseshoes, and keep-away were played with enthusiasm. And one old man, the variety store's janitor, wandered off with his fishing rod.

Every place she looked, Merry saw smiles on faces, and that was the way she liked it. Even Mrs. Fields graciously shared the recipe for her potato salad with the milkman's wife. Now that there was no trouble on his route, Mr. Wilson was everybody's friend.

Uncle Fred helped the boys lengthen the picnic table with sawhorses and boards. Even then there was not enough space for all the food. Mr. Wilson carried his ice-cream freezer to the shady tent of the willows. Tom trotted from the Tub to the freezer, not sure which held the biggest treat.

When sunset streaked the sky Penny knelt to

light the tepee of wood in the firepit. Flame leaped. The good smell of wood smoke sharpened appetites.

Older guests sat around the crowded table. Children spread blankets on the sand in the circle of firelight.

"Oh, Bill," Tina heard Aunt Anne say to Father. "This is like the picnics we had when we were children."

"It's perfect, isn't it?" Father answered warmly.

Tina smiled and watched rainbow color flick up from the heart of the bonfire. She felt safe when she overheard words which sprang out of family love.

The sky blackened. Stars dropped twinkling reflections on Lake Annabelle. People talked quietly.

Suddenly a rocket reached for heaven. In the far distance Yorkville's fireworks display shot the sky with golden sparks.

"Now!" Merry signaled Tina, Terry, and Jim Jackson.

Terry's flashlight cut a tunnel of light in the

night as the three crossed the beach to the boat dock.

"What *are* those children doing?" Merry heard Grandma ask Mother.

Merry hugged herself while she waited for the black lump of the Tub to move into the current of Lake Annabelle. Silently she ran to the willow clump and took her violin from its case. She returned to the outer circle around the fire. There she sat on a blanket with Tom, Penny, Mel and Butch.

Out on the lake a tiny flame was lowered to water level. "Ooh," Merry whispered, "don't go out. Please don't go out!"

"It won't," Tom said confidently.

Penny squeezed Merry's hand.

The little light grew in size, and another light was lowered. When a half dozen lights floated on the water, a gasp of pleasure rose from the group around the bonfire. As more lights were added, an elfin flotilla of sheer magic drifted in a moving curve. Each burning carton became a small ship, ablaze with light, headed for a far shore.

Merry tucked her violin under her chin. Softly she began to play one of Mother's favorites, "Now The Day Is Over." Almost instantly Mother began to sing. Aunt Anne's true alto blended. By the end of the verse, the whole group was singing. Merry's lashes dampened as the sweet, full tones echoed across the bay. Far in the distance she could see the black bulk of shoreline where the Arney house stood. Free of trouble, it waited for its share of summer happiness.

In a few minutes the dozens of floating fires would fade and Grandma would cut her red, white, and blue cake. Summer stretched ahead, to be filled with laughter and adventure.

But at this moment Father and Mother, Aunt Anne and Uncle Fred sat on opposite sides of the fire and sang. Grandpa rumbled in his throat and stroked Sugar's black head. Grandma beat time with her hands to amuse Jane Fields's baby. Penny left the blanket to check on Mr. Smith's comfort. Terry and Tina drifted in the Tub with Jim Jackson. Tom scurried away for another look at Mr. Wilson's ice-cream freezer. Toby's big feet kicked up sand when he ran after Tom.

Merry smiled at Butch and Mel and then began another song. There were Tuckers all over the place, and that was the way every Tucker liked it!

Whitman ADVENTURE
and MYSTERY Books